LAST DEFENSE

Harrisburg Railers, book 5

RJ SCOTT

V.L. LOCEY

Love Lane Books

Copyright

Deep Edge (Harrisburg Railers #5)

Copyright © 2017 RJ Scott, Copyright © 2017 V.L. Locey

Cover design by Meredith Russell, Edited by Sue Laybourn

Published by Love Lane Books Limited

ISBN - 9781785646225

All Rights Reserved

Dedication

To my family who accepts me and all my foibles and quirks.
Even the plastic banana in my holster.
VL Locey

Always for my family.
RJ Scott

Last DEFENSE

HARRISBURG RAILERS 5

RJ SCOTT & V.L. LOCEY

Love Lane Books

Chapter One

Ben

"No, see… that's not exactly the kind of… We're hoping to open up the search for more volunteers to help out over the summer." I leaned back in my chair, grimacing a bit when the old gal creaked loudly. The AC blowing into my face was measly but given I'd had it in that window for years and it had been donated, it was doing all I could ask of it. Papers shuffled about on my desk, the semi-cool air rustling over the mounds of paperwork that now fell to me. Gone were the days spent working with the animals at the Crossroads Shelter. Now I spent most of my time in this *damn* office, talking on the *damn* phone, trying to wheedle rich people into giving the shelter more of their money. It really kinda sucked.

Leaning back a bit more, I let my eyes drift shut.

Lenny, over at the Harrisburg Herald, rambled on and on about the cost of ads and how he didn't feel he could continue giving us a discount.

"No, we *do* understand. I need *you* to understand we need every penny of help we can get. We're a no-kill shelter. We're not state supported. Every dime— I know I tell you this all the time. That's because you complain about taking five percent off the cost of an ad every time I call."

Lenny prattled on a bit more about overheads.

Yeah, tell me about overheads, Lenny. I know all about them.

The harping turned into a droning noise, like Charlie Brown's teacher, and my mind began to wander. My gaze touched on the personal stuff practically buried under the piles of papers on my desk. A laptop with the shelter logo of a dog, a cat, and a human standing at a crossroads, bouncing around the screen. The laptop made a funny squeaking sound when I turned it on in the morning, but I ignored that. An empty coffee cup with the same logo on it, several books about miserable things like fundraising objectives and managerial and administrative duties in today's modern shelters, and a gay romance.

I picked up the book, flipped it open, and continued reading about a con man and a stripper who were working together to outfox some Mafiosi. The plot was a little weak, but the sex was hot, and, oh my stars, the romance was incredible. I missed romance. I missed that emotional connection to another man. I missed meaningful sex too. The few hookups I'd had since losing Liam had been cold and mechanical. I missed Liam so badly I ached. Yet I was too much of a coward to date. If I dated I might meet someone. And that someone might be perfect, as Liam had been. And that someone might marry me. And then that someone might die. No. No way was I capable of surviving that again. Better to have hollow fucks behind some gay club. That only hurt a little when the futility sank in.

Two years he'd been gone. My gaze left the romance novel and traveled to the picture that was almost obscured by stacks of folders. I reached over the debris and shoved the folders aside. Liam smiled at me from within the frame, his goofy face so endearing and special, and so beloved. Both of us had been hamming it up at the fundraiser it had been snapped at.

His blond hair glistened in the summer sun. Blue eyes sparkling. I was hanging off my husband, laughing like a fool, cradling Bucky, our new malamute pup, a shelter rescue of course. We'd had no idea then that within a month Liam would be dead. Multiple myeloma. Stage four bone cancer. He found a lump in his groin and three weeks later he was dead. At thirty-three years old. What the ever-loving fuck!? I mean, how did something like that even happen to a man that strong and vibrant?

"Yeah, no, I get it," I said after the long pause on the other end of the phone finally registered. I picked up the image of Liam and me in happier times and held it up in front of the AC. He'd always hated to be hot. Slept with a fan on all winter long. There I'd be under four layers of covers in long johns and wool socks, cussing about the icy wind blowing over us, and he'd just stretch those long athletic limbs out and sigh. Tennis players from Sweden were not right in the head.

"Stupid man, sleeping naked all winter," I mumbled wistfully. "Right, I get it. Just for another month? Thanks, Lenny. You're the best. Yeah, the standard plea for volunteers and helpers in the kennels. Kitten cuddlers, puppy smoochers—you know. Play up the fuzzy factor. Next week's paper sounds good. Thanks again."

I hung up before he could change his mind. Not that he would. I didn't think. I hoped. We were walking a financial tightrope now as it was. Having to shell out more for advertising to lure people in to work for free would mean one less paid staffer. And that was just not a doable thing. We only had one kennel manager, Diana Pierce, and an adoption counselor, Abby Barnes, on the payroll, and that was about all we could manage.

Our vet, Dr. Vince Owens, was a visiting vet who volunteered his time and never charged us unless it was something major that required surgery. Then the animal went to his office and we had to cough up the cash. Shots and routine stuff, Vince provided for free. And that was a real lifesaver. Paying for routine veterinary care would sink us, and the city really needed a no-kill shelter.

Sure, we had a big shelter over on the other side of the city, but they euthanized. A sad fact to be sure, and something that I hoped to avoid at all costs. If Crossroads closed, every dog and cat there would be shuttled across town. The majority would be put down, as they were older or had health issues. Hell, we were still trying to find homes for the old dogs people had dumped on our stoop last Christmas.

What kind of bastard dumps their old dog to make room for a Christmas puppy?

I was getting morose again. Time to get out of this stuffy box and maybe make the rounds. I pushed to my feet, stretched, and peeked around the desk at Bucky. Clear blue eyes blinked at me, his face resting on his front paws. Since malamute breeders cringe at blue eyes, we suspected that was why Bucky had been left outside a bar when he was about three weeks old. I guessed the breeder—rotten shit that he or she was—had seen those blue eyes and decided to get rid of that unwanted gene in a dumpster. Luckily for Bucky, Liam had found him, led to the trash receptacle by the whimpering, and brought him home to me.

"Morning, Winter Soldier," I whispered. His left

ear twitched. "You know your other dad named you something pretty amazing, right?"

He yawned, stretched, and slowly got to his feet. He knew he was kickass.

"Let's go see what the other dogs are doing this morning."

Bucky and I escaped the office for over an hour. Part of my job, aside from paperwork and groveling, was making sure all the animals were being treated humanely and that the facility was as clean as a whistle. Volunteers were saviors and angels in my book. Old women, college students, and those with gentle and loving hearts did some of the nastiest jobs in the shelter. You had to have a good heart to clean kennels and scoop litter boxes for nothing.

"Hey, boss."

I glanced over my shoulder to see Diana jogging toward me. She was the kennel manager, but her title also covered the "Cat House", a name we had wittily coined for the feline area.

My conversation with an old lab mix came to an end, but Bucky and the silver-muzzled black dog continued visiting.

"You have a call from Layton at the Railers," Diana said.

Layton Foxx worked on the social media for the Harrisburg Railers and we needed to discuss how the team and the shelter could work together.

"Is he on the line now?" I left the kennel, which

had been recently sanitized with pine disinfectant. I was aiming for the main office, which was where the public entered and began adoption proceedings.

"No, he said to call him when you had a minute. You think they're going to let us go to the arena with more dogs? That last visit netted us eight adoptions!"

Diana was a darling woman. Mid-forties, divorced, daughter in college. Short, kind of plump, curly brown hair cut short, and trustworthy. She was the only person in the shelter who knew the horrid details of Liam's last month. She'd suffered through his loss with me. And now, bless her, she felt she needed to guide me back into the world of romance.

"Yeah, that was a great idea. They seemed open to that becoming a regular thing, but since they're now in the playoffs, our visits are going to be limited."

"Well, he said he wanted to talk to you at your earliest."

I whistled for Bucky. "Maybe I'll just ride over to the arena."

"Office getting a bit claustrophobic?" She gave me a knowing look.

"Just a bit," I confessed, snapping a leash onto Bucky after he stopped the "WEARE-GOINGINTHECAR!" dance. "I'll be back in an hour. Call if anything massive happens."

She shoved me out the door. Bucky and I crossed the parking lot, stopping to chat with a family eying Fifi, a female poodle who had been bumped by a car

9

about two months ago. She was an older dog, and her healing had been slow, but now she was back in form and looking for a forever home.

After I directed the man and woman to the office, Bucky led me to my old Jeep Cherokee. We got him buckled in first, then I snapped the seat belt around my chest. I sniffed the air.

"Why does my Jeep smell like dog?" I looked at Bucky. He looked at me. "You need a bath."

He whined a bit. Bucky hated water but loved the snow. Snow could melt all over him and that was fine, but you fill up the tub and he was hiding behind the couch.

"Okay, so what do you want to listen to? Earth, Wind, & Fire, or Kool and the Gang?"

He picked EW&F. I could tell. Dog loved that band as much as I did.

Traffic was light this time of day. The morning commuters were where they needed to be, and lunch was a couple of hours off. I checked my phone, found nothing from my great-aunts, whispered a thanks to the Big Guy, and turned up *The Best of Earth, Wind, and Fire*.

Cruising to the north side of town, jamming and singing, I pulled into the East River Arena and parked by the same door I had used when I'd been there before. There were no people to be seen, just cars, some pretty damn expensive.

"Bet that Jag over there doesn't smell like dog," I

mentioned to Bucky. He sneezed. "Oh hell, *Shining Star.*"

Damn, but I loved this song. I cranked the volume up and started seat-dancing. I would have gotten out and danced, since I was a pretty good dancer, but seat-dancing and singing would have to suffice. I liked singing too. Pastor Bert at my church thought I had a fine voice. Course, he said that to everyone in the choir, but I took it to heart.

I was belting out the lyrics, the windows down, enjoying the living hell out of my hour of office freedom. Someone slapped me on the arm through my open window. It hurt. I mean, like it really hurt. I threw a look to the left, and there stood the huge Russian I'd met a couple of times previously. Stan. The Railers' goalie. He was grinning widely.

"I make dance too! Like Dick Clark!"

I gaped at the moose shaking his ass all over the parking lot. The man with him, a leaner guy with a head of blond curls, chuckled at him but never once asked him to stop.

"I am making milkshake to bring boys for to my yard," Stan yelled.

That one got me, and I laughed out loud. Bucky barked loudly, picking up the happy vibes.

"Dude, you are for sure going to have all kinds of boys in your yard," I told Stan after I'd exited my Jeep and had Bucky's leash in hand.

"Thank you. I am good with shaking money

maker. Is this dog for us?" Stan crouched down to run his fingers over Bucky's soft head.

"Stan, we really can't do a dog yet," the blond said.

"Oh, well no, but soon. We win Cup and then make dog. Big one. Like this, but ugly with long teeth."

"I'm not sure we can find you an ugly dog with long teeth," I confessed.

"Yeah, we're not looking for an ugly dog. Stan," the blond said, and extended his hand. We shook, then he led Stan off, fingers linked with the big Russian's. Well, huh. Gay people were just all *over* the place. I did recall reading about Tennant Rowe coming out but had never heard anything about the goalie. I wasn't a huge Railers fan. My heart was with the Washington hockey team, since I'd been born and raised in D.C. and only moved here after college to keep an eye on my two elderly great-aunts.

Aunts who were awfully quiet today.

I checked my phone again, saw nothing from the police or the neighbors, and decided to enjoy a peaceful and tranquil day.

"Nice dog." I paused just this side of the players' entrance at the deep voice coming from behind me. There was something about that man's voice…the timbre of the bass or the way he spoke. Not sure what it was, but the last time he'd spoken to me my body had had the same kind of reaction. A spear of latent heat low in my belly followed by a shiv of icy dread.

"Thanks." I wanted to stare at the door. Or run. I couldn't do either of those, though, so I turned to face the bearded man. Christ, but he was fierce-looking. Like a Viking, with piercing eyes and an aura that screamed berserker. He was bigger than me. Taller by at least four inches and probably sixty pounds. He was wearing a suit, as Stan and Erik had been, but his looked incredibly fine on his burly frame. Dark blue with a silver tie and a white shirt. His biceps strained the material trying to contain them.

"His name is Bucky." There now, I had spoken to the man who made my heart leap around inside my chest like a frog on a highway.

"Like Captain America's sidekick?" He looked down at my worn T-shirt with Cap's shield on it.

"Exactly like that."

He took another step, which put him into my little personal space bubble, his gaze and mine locked. I wet my lips and jerked my chin up a bit. I wasn't going to let some hockey player intimidate me.

"Cute dog. Hot owner." He gave me a long, slow look, petted Bucky, and stepped around the dull-witted man trying to digest the fact Mr. Fear had said he was hot. "Are you coming in, or are you teaching your dog to open doors mentally?"

"I'm here to see Layton Foxx."

"Yeah? Well, I'm here to participate in morning skate."

"I know who you are. Max van Hellren. You played for Washington four years ago."

He tugged the door open and settled a kind of bored look on me. "Yeah, that was me. You like Washington?"

"Hometown team." Bucky barked to back me up. Max smiled. All the ferocity that oozed out of him dissipated when he smiled. The man was seriously fine.

"Maybe I can change your mind about which team to cheer for, Mr. Washington Fan."

"Ben. My name is Ben."

He nodded just once, his hand still keeping the door open. "Ben. I like that. Suits you. So, are we coming in or are we going to flirt here in front of Pete?"

A security guard peeked around the door and winked at me. I wanted to die. Right there.

"I don't flirt," I snapped. I stalked around Max and Pete and went off to find Layton Foxx. Determination hot in my breast kept me from looking back to see if Max was checking out my ass. I hoped he was and I prayed he wasn't.

Chapter Two

Max

I followed Tall Dark and Gorgeous into the arena, kind of disappointed when he turned left, heading for the admin offices, and I had to carry on into the bowels of the arena and the locker rooms. I wasn't stupid; there was a spark there with Ben-the-Washington-Fan, and you know, love is love, and sex is sex, and I'd surely like some of the latter with him. Of course, he'd have to leave his dog outside the room, but we could work around that.

Still, it didn't matter. This was the Railers, the biggest rainbow-flag-flying team in the history of the NHL, I wasn't one to go around flirting with strangers in front of people who might see me. I had a reputation as a hard guy to uphold, and flirting was a hundred kinds of soft and sexy and hot.

"A word?" Coach Madsen asked as he stepped out from the shadows. As if he'd been waiting for me.

"I'm not late," I said, and looked at my watch just to check. As soon as I saw I was in fact at least an hour early, I felt a familiar dread seep into me and I had to stop myself from pressing a hand to my head.

No one knows. No one will ever know.

Coach Madsen, or Mads as we called him on the team, frowned at my exaggerated reaction. "No, jeez, cool your jets—I'm not a school principal, and you're not late. I just wanted to go over some video with you from Saturday's game."

Relief flooded into me as quickly as dread had, and yet again I was in the position of having to look as if nothing in the world worried me at all. I wouldn't have to lie for very much longer; this was my last year in hockey. I knew it, Coach Madsen knew it; hell, the entire NHL was painfully and vocally aware this defenseman, over thirty now, was on his last hurrah on an expansion team.

Never mind the Railers had made it to the first round of the Stanley Cup, the gleaming goal for any hockey player, I was still a man on his way out on a team that still hadn't shown exactly how far they could go in the standings. Last year they'd made it this far and been knocked out. This year they had me.

Oh, and wonder boy Ten, also Toly, Dieter, and poor Arvy at home with a fucked knee, and Stan in goal, and…yeah, it wasn't just me, but anyone who looked at my record would be able to see I could make a difference.

If I don't collapse and die on the ice first.

Way to be melodramatic.

"Okay, Coach, we can do that. You want to do it after practice?"

"It was just one thing—come in now," Mads said, and began walking toward the office he shared with the goalie coach. He expected me to follow, and I did. I respected the hell out of Jared Madsen. A solid defenseman, he would have gone all the way on a team that loved him if it hadn't been for a heart issue. He'd chosen to stop then, wanting more from life than the rush of playing. But then he'd found Ten, so he was okay, living his dream vicariously through his lover and being the best D-coach I'd ever had the fortune to play for.

Why would I want to give up skating, even with my issues? I had no one to replenish the gap that skating filled. I had glory and success in my future, and nothing was getting in my way.

Although I wouldn't mind the odd pit-stop with a strong, sexy, cute, dog-owning man who'd caught my eye.

Mads sat at his desk and swung his chair around, pressing a button to start the VT.

"This," he said, and pointed at the screen.

It was another Flyers game. All we'd done was watch game tapes over the last few weeks since we'd captured our place in the finals. We'd drawn the Philly team as our opponent and needed to get as much information as we could to make our game plans. Coach Benton was all about the process, about playing the game and not worrying about tricks from the other team. His mantra was that we played right and we'd have a greater chance to win.

But we all wanted that edge; that one small thing that could light the lamp.

"See?" Mads gestured with a laser pointer. "See how they lose control on the rebound here? If you could get in, you could collect that and shuttle it up without losing sight of Ten."

"Play it again." I sat on the corner of his desk, making sure not to put my entire weight there in case the damn thing collapsed. I wasn't one of those D-men who were light on their feet and all about finessing the puck off the other team's offense. I was the grinder, the heavyweight who wasn't afraid to take punches and give them straight back. I was an instigator, a defender, the man who could take a lagging game and give the team the impetus to fight back. A throwback to the old and bad days of hockey, and every team needed someone like me when they had generational phenoms like Ten on their team.

I was good at what I did, and the problem there is that when you're really good at what you do as a D-man, you get sent out against the opponents' most skilled scorers. Damn, it's hard to keep up with some of them. Like Ten for instance, although luckily for me I was on his team now.

The coaches put me with Ten, I had his back, and for that I knew Jared respected me.

I thrived on that, on respect, being the hero, hearing the roar of the crowd and knowing they loved what I was doing for *their* team.

Christ knew what I would do when this was over. I couldn't be a coach, not like Mads. I'd want to be on the ice all the time, muscling my way through another game.

"So, what do you think?" Mads asked as he played it for the third time. I could see what he was showing me, and I needed to get my head out of thinking about the next part of my sorry life and focus on the here and now. Here was the arena; now was our upcoming first game against the Flyers.

"I think they should tone down the orange," I quipped, in reference to the brightness of the Flyers' gear.

"About the—"

"I know what you mean, I can see it, I'll work on it." And then because this was Ten I would be looking out for, I added what I knew Mads wanted to hear. "I'll get to the puck but I won't let them get to Ten."

"I wasn't worried about that," he lied to my face.

"Of course not," I lied back.

That was how we rolled.

. . .

WHEN I LEFT the small office, heading for the locker rooms, I came face to face with Stan on his hands and knees, in his full goalie kit, ass in the air, fussing over the dog Ben had brought in with him. No sign of Ben at the moment.

Stan spoke Russian to the dog, who had rolled on its back, exposing its belly for a rub. I made out one word, the name Noah, then a lot more curiously shaped vowels and consonants that meant nothing to me.

I'd played with a hundred Russians in my time, and they all had a place in my heart, these big strong guys with the weird language that made no sense to me at all.

"You like?" Stan asked, and I realized he was looking up at me, the big goofy idiot.

"Dogs?" I asked, and crouched down to fuss over Bucky as I'd overheard Ben call him. He was soft, and warm, and reminded me of this mutt we had when I was a kid, a collie lab mix who had never left my side. I'm not ashamed to admit when Scooter died at eleven, I cried for days. I was already in the draft, called up for the AHL team attached to the Hawks, but I cried like a baby for the dog who had been mine.

"I love dogs," I said, simple and to the point.

"I'm steal him," Stan joked. "Not tell Erik."

I stood up and smiled down at the Russian and the dog he wanted to steal. "Think Ben might have something to say to that."

Talk of the devil and there he was, with Layton Foxx at his side. Truth, I'd never seen such a fine-looking pair of men standing together.

I really need to find someone to scratch this itch. I need to get laid soon, before I spontaneously combust.

"There he is," Ben said, and reached for the leash. "I take my eye off him for one minute…"

Stan looked so disappointed Ben was there taking the dog it was comical. I didn't want to laugh but it just happened.

Stan huffed and stalked away, and that left me with Ben, Layton, and the dog in the lonely corridor.

"We meet again," I said to Ben, then groaned inwardly. *Lame.* My game was so not on point.

I eased past Ben, which was a tight fit, and sue me if I didn't press a little more that I needed to on his arm. He stepped back, nearly falling over Bucky, and I gripped him to stop him from barreling into Layton. Call it a hockey instinct, or just a need to get my hands on him. Who knows, but I was there, and I held him until he shrugged me off. He glared at me, then pointedly turned his back to me.

"So, this would be all the team for the calendar, or can I pick who I want?" he said to Layton, as they walked away talking. I heard my name, and a chuckle from Layton, before they headed out to the kitchen.

"Heads up," someone shouted, and I only just ducked in time to avoid getting a soccer ball to my head. I retrieved the ball and threw it back to Westy and Mac.

"Stupid rookies," I muttered, and muscled my way through, ignoring their laughter as much as I'd ignored Ben and Layton's.

No one laughed at the big bad defender.

And when I took both rookies to the floor at the beginning of practice, I felt vindicated when I saw in their eyes that it was a lesson from me.

If only I could get Ben on the floor under me, all wriggling and cursing at me.

Now that would be a Very Good Thing.

Practice was hard. Our first game in the finals was on the Flyers' home ice, which meant a plane, and hotels, and messing with the rhythms of our day. We'd deal with all that; at the end of the day, it was all about the hockey.

Ten cornered me, as much as you can corner someone on an oval piece of ice.

"Did Mads show you the—"

"Yes."

"And did you—"

"Yes."

"Okay then."

We fist-bumped, because we just got each other. I've seen a lot of kids come up and be labelled the next great one when they were still wet behind the ears, but Ten here, he had hockey smarts, and speed, and everyone genuinely liked him.

Well, except for the section of the Railers' fans that felt Ten was defined by what he did with his dick. Morons.

I'd already heard some of the chirping he got from certain skaters on opposing teams, just enough to inform me which assholes I was taking off their skates into the boards. No one said things loud enough to get caught, no one spoke clearly, but nevertheless it was an easy go-to thing to comment on a man's sexuality.

I preferred using my brawn over my brain when it came to getting things done.

Didn't mean I was short of a brain, though.

Just that my brain had this thing in it, and it wasn't good, and I didn't even want to think about it.

"Again," Mads said, and had me and James "Westy" Sato-West, a newbie up from the minors, going two-on-one with Ten. Little shit still got past the both of us, a slap shot to the net, and not even Stan could stop that one.

Ten crowed a little—he'd earned that—and then he snowed to a stop right next to me.

"Better luck next time," he said with a grin.

"Little shit," I cursed, but I was smiling, because fuck I felt alive out here.

We finished with what I affectionately called circle time, all of us around the inner Railers' logo on the ice, all taking a knee and listening to assessments and timetables.

We were flying out the day after tomorrow. Flight left at five p.m. Hotel was assigned. Optional practice in the Flyers' place the morning of the game. We were told to skip the ice tomorrow, spend our time in the gym, work with the therapists on any lingering issues, and then be ready to fly out.

Some of the guys were beaten and bruised after the end of a heavy season; we all needed some TLC, but I wished we could have got the skate time tomorrow, early, when the ice was new and maybe I was the only one out on it.

Just me, the ice, and the echoing ghosts of the cheers from the last game.

I was the last off the ice. It was kind of a thing I had going on at all my teams; it didn't bother me when I got on the ice and in what order, there was no superstition there, but leaving the ice at practice? That was all me being last.

God knows why. Maybe it was that part of me that said if I wore the same shirt on game day, or a particular tie to a game against LA, then we would win. Hockey superstition is a weird thing.

I saw him before he saw me, or at least, he was staring off in the other direction, making shapes with his hands as he talked to Layton, who was grinning at him as if Ben was telling him the best joke ever.

I wanted to walk over and see if they were still

laughing about me, but I didn't.

Not at first, anyway. Only when Layton answered his cell and that left Ben on his own did I think about culling him from the herd.

I used all my best moves, coming up on his blind side, nearly tripping over the dog, and sliding effortlessly between Ben and Layton, who took his call a little farther away.

Me and Ben. Alone. Finally.

"We should get coffee. Or beer. Or a hotel room," I announced, because hell, life was too short to mess around. Ben could say yes or punch me in the face, and either I could handle.

"You just don't take a hint, do you?" he said, and wrapped Bucky's leash around his hand, ready to move off.

"You know you find me hot."

"Jesus, you're an arrogant ass——"

I leaned in to him. "I don't mess about. You're fucking gorgeous and I want to fuck you into tomorrow."

"What if I want to be the one doing the fucking?" he snapped, then blanched when he realized what he'd said.

God, I was so hard my cup was cutting off circulation. The idea of this man getting it on and taking charge was exactly my kind of thing.

"I can go for that," I whispered.

"Why are you messing with me like this?" he

asked, horrified, and looked around him. "Is this some kind of sick joke? A game?"

"No joke, and Ben, I don't play games," I said.

Something in that must have resonated with him because he stopped in his tracks and there was something in his expression—a hope, a need—and it was the same as mine.

"Max—"

"I'll be at Blue. It's a bar on—"

"I know where it is."

"I'll be there at eight. Your choice."

I didn't give him any time to discuss or argue. The offer was there—we met at Blue, we had a drink, we talked, maybe we had sex up against a wall. Either way, I'd found the way in to this beautiful man's mind. A simple promise I didn't play games.

"Wait," he called after me as I headed for the lockers. I didn't stop. I'd laid it out there, and now it was on him what happened next.

Chapter Three

Ben

L ongest. Day. Ever.

I'd spent hours debating and whining, bouncing back and forth over whether I should meet Max or not. It had taken me until four o'clock to slap myself and make the call. Yes. Drinks with the big man who looked at me as if I was filet mignon. Why? Because there was a current, sharp and hot, and it had been years since I'd felt that kind of spark.

Getting out of the office at six—an hour past my "official" quitting time, which I never actually saw because *shelter manager*—added another sixty minutes to the torture.

"What do I say to him when I show up?"

You say you want to fuck him until he passes out. Then

fuck him—or have him fuck you—until you or he passes out. Simpleton.

"That really wasn't a question I needed answered, brain." Bucky glanced over at me as we made our way to Allison Hill and the red brick row houses me and my two great-aunts called home. "Talking to myself. Go back to what you were doing."

The malamute gave me a knowing look and returned to his previous entertainment, which was riding along with his snout out the six-inch dog-nose-sized gap in the window, slobber flying off him on occasion to coat said window and speckle my arm.

Pulling up to a red light, I glanced at the clock on the stereo. Quarter after six. Why was I so obsessed with time today?

You know why.

"Okay, seriously, I will shut your shit down, brain!" Bucky rolled those blue eyes toward me, the whiskers over his eyes twitching in what seemed to be amusement. "It's not funny."

No, it was not funny. Not at all. I'd made an ass of myself over a man. That hadn't happened since... forever. Since Liam.

"Right, so what we're going to do is just meet for drinks. No fucking."

Bucky woofed out the window.

"No, see, fucking is for the nameless men. Max has a name. Well, okay, yeah, the other men did too, but they didn't make me feel as if I'd swallowed live goldfish when I thought about them."

The light turned green just as I cranked up the volume on some slow stuff from Lionel Ritchie. We drove as I talked. When I came out of the conversational fog, we were about four blocks from my street. I shook off the spike of fear I'd felt after realizing I'd driven for ten minutes and not once noted my surroundings. I'd get myself killed over a man with whiskey-colored eyes and a voice like a chainsaw on idle.

Allison Hill was a rough neighborhood or had been. It still was in pockets, but there were now areas that had been gentrified. And then, on the south side of Allison Hill, there were abandoned houses filled with squatters, many with addicts who slept on beds of empty syringes and shattered dreams.

The bad side of the city was why I'd moved up after I'd gotten that spiffy major in business administration with a minor in animal science. My two great-aunts on my father's side had lived there all their lives. When crime had started taking over their neighborhood, instead of moving down to D.C. with my parents as they'd been begged to do, they'd simply dug in like ticks and begun speaking out for the people of the area. That had brought them a lot of trouble from criminal elements who didn't want the streets cleaned up. Enter Benton Worthington, nephew extraordinaire and bail-payer for two wild women who should be home knitting and baking cookies instead of playing social justice warriors in their late seventies and early eighties.

The job offer from Crossroads had come before I'd even fully moved in, which had been a miracle, but one didn't question blessings. They just thanked God for them.

And I had every day for the past several years. My job, Liam, good health, and a full life had been in my grasp. Life had been good. So good that I'd been rapidly promoted. Only two years after I'd become shelter manager, the owner, who had been aged and sickly, had offered Liam and me the shelter. We'd talked, plotted, begged, borrowed, and came close to stealing to raise the down payment. Legally, all had been settled after the transfer of ownership had taken place. Our wills had both stated that should one of us die before the other, the shelter went to the surviving spouse. Little had we suspected that one of us would be gone within a few years.

When Liam had died, the sunny gloss had faded from my existence. So had passion and feeling and the hot lick of attraction for another man. All gone. Until I'd gone and looked into Max van Hellren's eyes and seen fire and life there.

Bucky whimpered, and I stared at our house while moving past.

"Shit. Next time *tell* me I drove past our place

before I drive past it. Sorry, not your fault. Totally on me."

Bucky's tail thumped against the seat. I circled the block, parked in my designated slot in front of the row of townhomes, and unbuckled my dog. He leaped out of the Jeep and trotted to number 20, knowing we'd go check on the old gals before entering our own small house.

My aunts were in the kitchen, at the table, the small kitchen smelling of coffee and rebellion.

"What are we protesting this week?" I asked, giving each of the short women a kiss on a leathery cheek. Both were gray, wrinkled, and as lean as whip pets. Neither had ever married, and they had never borne any children.

"Unfair wages," replied Aunt Carol—the youngest, at seventy-seven—as her brush moved with confidence over the blank top of a picket sign.

"That prick Senator Rudy wants to vote down a raise in the minimum wage. Don't those rich politicians know that a higher minimum wage will mean poor people can buy more goods, which will help small businesses and lower crime since stealing and robbing folks isn't needed if you can earn a decent living?" Aunt Glenna—the older at eighty-one—waved a hand at the microwave. "There's a plate of pork chops and scalloped potatoes for you."

"Thanks, but I grabbed something at work." That was a lie—I hadn't eaten since breakfast. My stomach was too knotted to eat. I stole a look at the clock on the wall. Ten after seven. I had to get a move on or risk being late.

"If you're free on Saturday, come march with us," Carol said, tongue between teeth as she painted some sort of slogan on her sign. I began inching toward the back door.

"Yeah, come join us as we stick it to the man," Glenna chimed in, then stapled some poster board to a slat of wood.

"I'm pretty sure no one says 'the man' anymore," I commented, my eyes darting back to the clock. "And if I go and get arrested, who will bail your backsides out?"

"He makes a good point," Carol said as she painted.

"You okay, baby? You look off." Glenna reached out to take my hand.

I gave her a wobbly smile. "Just low blood sugar."

They both stopped making signs and gave me that look. The one that was stuffed with frustration.

"Benton, baby, have you been running too hard again?" Carol looked at me through paint-smeared bifocals. "You know all that jogging during the summer makes you faint."

"Once. That happened one time." I held up a finger, then slid toward the door, Bucky waiting with his nose flat to the screen in the door. "And that was only because I didn't hydrate properly. I have to run to stay in shape. My job has me behind a desk for…" I sighed. I gave up. We'd been over my need to jog a thousand times. There was no changing some minds.

Both old women gave me surly looks.

"I have to go out tonight. Can you check on Bucky in a couple of hours and let him out? Thanks. Night!"

I ran out, tripped over the dog, and nearly went on my nose.

"Where are you heading to, Benton?"

"Is it a date?"

God above, save me from old women. "Just a meeting. About dog crates."

I grabbed Bucky's leash, and we hightailed it next door.

My skinny house was stuffy. Bucky ate dinner, then curled up on the bed to nap while I opened the windows, showered, shaved, and tried to find clothes that said I was maybe interested but not madly in lust.

"So, clothes that lie," I said to my reflection in the mirror that hung on the back of the closet door. I settled on a short-sleeved cotton shirt, soft blue, one Liam had said was my color. Then jeans, clean but not pressed, and some loafers. Maybe a watch? I yanked open my underwear drawer, and there it was. The small soft square of velvet that I'd wrapped my wedding band in just two months ago.

Suddenly I felt traitorous. I sat on the bed beside Bucky, gently opening the folded swatch. The thin gold band blinked at me in the late day sun. I slid it on, eyes closing, memories rushing over me. The day Liam had proposed right after we'd graduated college, our frantic plans to get up into Canada to get married, and the sheer joy of the day we exchanged bands and vows. Rubbing my finger over the smooth circlet of gold, I could see Liam's brother Rolf storming into the small venue we'd rented upon coming back to the States. Rolf, the sneering hateful bigot who never could decide what sickened him the most: his brother marrying a *fag* or his brother marrying, in his words, a *black* fag. Only he didn't use the word black, but loved throwing the most offensive terms he could to describe the color of my skin. Never mind Liam was also gay. It was all me. I had led his baby brother astray.

"Man was a flaming jackass," I told Bucky. My dog rolled onto his back, so I rubbed his belly for a moment, letting the memories fade away just a bit. The dog dozed off, and I glanced at the clock beside the bed.

"Shit." I rushed from the bedroom, grabbed my wallet and keys from the side table by the front door, and slid out, promising Bucky I'd be home in an hour.

I cruised into Blue's parking lot on South Cameron Street nearly thirty minutes later. Parking was a hassle, but I finally found a slot around back. I inhaled, exhaled, and let the dulcet tones of The Miracles wash over me.

"Right. Drinks with a sexy man. You got this, Benton."

The moment I entered the bar I could feel those predatory eyes on me. It felt as if cougars had spotted a newborn lamb bounding across the pasture.

Max watched me walk to him, sipping from a tumbler that held something amber. The tables were full, as were the booths along the wall, where Max held the last one by the jukebox.

"I thought you were going to blow this off," Max said as I sat down across from him in the wide booth.

"Had to work late."

He waved at the bartender as he sipped. His tongue darted out to grab a small droplet of liquid, the sight spearing me in the groin, unfurling into hot fingers of lust.

"Whiskey and water," I told the barkeep. Max looked pleased with my drink choice.

"Glad you came," he said, his gaze roaming over me as a smile worked along his lips, pulling up the corners then fading. "So, you go and get married since this morning?"

My eyebrows knotted, then I remembered the band on my finger. "Oh, uh, no. I was just trying it on and forgot to take it off."

"Planning on getting married, then?" His demeanor seemed chilly now.

"No, I *was* married. He died. I was feeling…" I leaned back to let the bartender place my drink in front of me. I paid, and the barkeep left. "I'm not sure what I was feeling."

"I'm sorry for your loss." He sounded sincere. I nodded, picked up my drink, and met his gaze. "You sure you're into this?"

I drained my glass. "I thought we could maybe talk. Get to know each other."

"If that's really what you want? I mean, if that's what you came here for, then I'm happy to shoot the shit, but what I'm feeling simmering between us hasn't got much to do with talking."

A shiver of want skittered over my flesh. He was right. He was wrong. He was too damn masculine to be real.

I slid out of the long seat, my gaze locked with his. He followed me out the door, neither of us saying a thing until we stood by my Cherokee. Then I turned to look at him.

"I thought we could maybe talk out here. See, there's this spark…"

He reached for me, massive hand latching onto the back of my neck. The kiss was rough, hungry, fierce. Kind of like how he played hockey. It stole my breath, and my senses as well it seemed, because somehow, as tongues tangled and teeth scraped, we managed to fall into my car. There was no way we had enough room. We were behind a damn bar. People could walk out and see us. Didn't stop us. I guess neither of us had much sense.

"Shut the door," I panted as we broke apart in the mad rush to touch each other. He did, thankfully not on anyone's leg. Max was under me, his hands now pushing at my shirt, shoving it up to bare my chest. As his mouth settled over my left nipple, I found the lever and the seat slammed back as far as it would go.

"You taste like pure sin," he murmured, then tugged soundly on my nipple. My spine tightened. I rotated my hips after my legs settled on either side of him. Stiff cock moved over stiff cock. He inhaled, pulling cooler air over my already sensitive nipple. "Turn around."

"No. What? Oh shit." He was shoving at me roughly. Our legs were far too long for this shit, but we managed to untangle ourselves. I leaned in to suckle on his mouth before facing forward. He was hot single malt whisky on my tongue. His thick beard scratched my face. Kissing. I'd not done this since Liam had been alive. The hookups? No, no kissing for them. That made things too personal, I guessed. I'd missed the taste and pressure of a man's mouth on mine.

He was forceful but gentle, if that makes sense. Pushing and pulling, wild to get me how he wanted me yet never making me feel caged. "Get these down."

Hands on my hips, he yanked my pants down, taking my best boxer briefs down with them. God above, it was getting stuffy in this car. His hands roamed over my ass, fondling the tight orbs, his skin calloused and scratchy. Perfect.

"Need a condom." He lifted himself as if reaching into a back pocket.

I jerked and pulled until I had one leg free, then I leaned up, arms over the dash, ass open and needy. Hearing him rip open a condom packet then spit onto his hand had me whimpering.

"Yes…hell fire, yes," I mewled, fingers grasping at the dashboard while he eased me back into position. He spat again. My eyes rolled back into my head. Sweat beaded on my brow and upper lip.

"Sit back on me, Ben. Easy. Fuck. Oh fuck, you should see this…"

It took all I had not to faint from the sheer delight of a man's fat cock breaching me.

"Your ass is perfect. Yeah, good, sit down now. Easy, easy. So hot." He thrust upward, driving his cock so far into me I yelped, then groaned. "Ride me. Hard. Yeah, good man. Fuck yeah. Good man."

With his fingers biting into my hips, we fucked like beasts, my chest thumping into the dash when he drove up into me, his knee slapping the door each time I dropped to impale myself. We paused a few times for him to spit on his hand and spread the spittle on his cock, then I was back on him, eager as hell for the stretch and burn.

"You close?"

"Yeah," I huffed while rolling my ass in circles, his

dick deeply embedded in me. Max made this guttural sound every time I did that. I did too.

He slid a sweaty arm around me, hoisting me up. My head slammed into the roof, then I arched back to lie on him, arms locked overhead, hands splayed on the headliner fabric.

"Just sit there and move your hips as you do." His voice was even grittier now. He fisted my cock. "Fuck but you're juicy," he murmured into my skin as he worked precum over the head of my prick. "Come for me now. Sit still. Come for me and let your sweet ass sucking and grabbing me pull me over. Do it. Let go, Ben. Yeah, that's it, baby. Fuck yeah. Shit. Ah, shit."

The orgasm came quickly. I shot hot and violently, garbled sounds that were barely human burbling out of me. He held me tight to him with his left hand, his hold slightly painful, which made the release that much better.

His teeth found the nape of my neck, and he latched on as he came. Writhing, slick with sweat and covered with my own cum, I squeezed tightly, grabbing his kicking cock internally, milking him wantonly.

"Ah hell," I gasped, spent and soaked with sweat and semen, my muscles contracting then loosening over and over.

"Fucking beautiful man," Max growled beside my ear as the mating frenzy abated.

There I sat—lay, whatever—my back on his chest,

his cock so far inside me that drawing deep breaths was hard, eyes closed, blissed out.

"I think I came on the dash," I finally blurted out. Max chuckled. It was a dirty little laugh that made me smile. Fuck, but that had been fantastic. Messy. Messy. Oh fuck. So messy and sweaty and rough, just as sex should be. "We never talked about our status."

That kind of cut through the rosy afterglow. Max muttered something against my shoulder, licked a hot path up my sweaty neck, then eased me up off him.

"Sorry, yeah, things kind of got stupid."

I fell into the driver's side, my pants dangling off one leg, my ass over the console. I tensed for a second when I felt his fingers slipping down the crack of my ass. He rubbed at my hole with two fat fingers, working them into me. I shuddered and pushed back against those digits, begging for more of him in me. Fingers, dick, tongue—didn't matter. As long as he got inside me again.

"I'm negative. Always careful," he said.

"Mm, mmm." I couldn't speak while he was fingering me so gently.

"Like that?"

"Yeah, so much. Me too. Negative. Use another finger."

I got that raunchy chuckle again, then, sadly, he pulled out and gave my ass a loving little pat.

"Let's go somewhere private. With some air."

"I can do air." I wiggled into the seat, rolled this

way and that until I had my pants up over my ass and was sitting up facing the wheel. Max leaned over the console and kissed me, his hand falling to my cock still out in the air. "Need keys."

"My place is close. I have stuff. Lube. Condoms. Toys. I'm easy. I just need more of you."

"Where are my keys?!" I dug into my front pockets. My phone slid to the floor and started ringing. "Oh man, no…" I groaned as the familiar ringtone of a friend of mine—a fine member of the Harrisburg Police Department—filled the car. "I have to take that.'

"Okay, take it." He flopped back into his seat, his hand still cradling my cock.

I placed the phone to my ear. "Dwayne, if my aunts are in lockup tell them I'll be there in an hour."

"Make it three," Max said, hand still stroking my cock back to life.

"Three hours. Tell them I'll be there in three—"

"Ben, it's not your aunts. It's the shelter. It's been vandalized. The glass in the front door is busted in. Someone passing by saw it and called it in the same time the alarm from the security system rang through. We need you down here to tell us if anything has been stolen."

"Dammit!" I threw a look at Max, who decided things weren't going as we would have liked, so he dropped my cock. "Okay, I'll be there in thirty. Thanks, Dwayne."

"Any time, man."

I hung up on the cop who'd adopted two of my older dogs for his kids.

"Trouble?"

Keys now in hand, I cranked the Jeep over, eager for the rush of stale but cool air.

"Shelter issues. Vandals. I have to go." I looked to the right, sure he'd be pissed, but he seemed cool. Sweaty, and still with his big soft dick out, but cool.

"You want to do this again?" he asked.

"Can we make it to a bed next time?"

"Yeah, we can do that."

We tucked and zipped, and then I reached for him. My mouth took his, and he responded with passion. When we parted, his gaze was smoldering again.

"Give me your phone."

I didn't argue and watched as he typed in some numbers, took a selfie as the contact picture, sent himself a message, and handed it back to me.

"Now we have each other's numbers. I'll call when we're back from Philly, beautiful man." He patted my face, softly, then left the Jeep, closing the door and disappearing.

"Sweet baby Jesus," I whispered, taking just a moment to try to work on a face that wouldn't show the cops I'd just been fucked senseless in a parking lot. I needed more AC. Stat.

Chapter Four

Max

Coach Benton wasn't moving. He didn't walk up and down the locker room like my last head coach. He didn't curse at us like the one I had before that, even. After twelve years in the league and seven different teams, I'd seen coaches pace, scream, throw things, and even cry. But Coach Benton was a whole new ballgame.

"So, we lost," he summarized, quietly, controlled, his hands loose at his sides.

Yep. Too right we fucking lost.

All tied at three goals each, then the Flyers had got one past us twenty-three seconds into overtime. I'd been on the damn ice. It was me they'd got a goal past.

Now Coach would lose it, and I glanced at Mads,

43

the defensive coach, who stood, arms crossed over his chest, just watching the room. I couldn't get a fix on him either. I'd have thought he'd be consoling Ten, who was slumped in his stall looking as if someone had stolen all his toys and burned them in front of him.

"This is game one," Coach continued. "We're here again in two days, and we can win. We played a good game tonight; I saw a lot of smart moves out there."

And then he left, and Mads followed him, as did the other assistants, and Julio the equipment guy, who exchanged looks with me as he went out.

I'd spent time on the plane yesterday talking to Julio. After all this time in the NHL, with my experience on varied teams, I knew the first person you made friends with was the guy in charge of the equipment. Leave coffees, Danishes, gifts, and leave them at the skate-sharpening altar, and they will respect that you respect them.

Julio was retiring this year; he'd seen as much as I had, but he was in his mid-sixties, and gray. I was only thirty, yet retirement was only the remainder of the season away.

If I made it that far.

Our captain stood up. Connor was not only a brilliant player, but he had this way about him that commanded respect. He didn't take any shit and he wouldn't let us leave this room until we'd talked this through.

"That was bad luck," he said, and everyone nodded. We all knew we'd played well, and apart from one lucky bounce we could have battled back up the ice to their goal and maybe it would have been us with the win. His glance landed on me, then on my defensive partner, Westy. "This is not on you two," he said. Then he looked deliberately at Ten, Ads and Larson, in turn. "Nor you. Just because the goal went in on your shift, this is not your shit to carry."

Ten nodded, and I was nodding as well.

"Now, let's get back to the hotel, get some food and sleep, and we're back here tomorrow for practice."

Out of the corner of my eye, I saw Dieter raise his hand, as if he was in school. I heard a couple of people groan at the move.

"Lola is here with Trent."

"You're joking," Ten said with an exaggerated groan to end. "Not Lola. Last time she sat with us, I couldn't feel my cheek for a week where she pinched it. And I don't mean the cheek on my face."

Everyone else laughed. This was clearly some kind of long-running joke I hadn't been part of— before I'd been traded in.

"I can't help it," Dieter defended himself, and looked aggrieved. "She's part of the package."

"Who is?" I asked Westy.

"Trent's grandmother. She came up with Trent for the game."

"Why is that a problem?"

Westy side-eyed me. "You'll see."

We showered, changed, and were back on the coach in good time. Traveling to the hotel took maybe fifteen minutes, and it was one hell of a place. All polished marble and glass, it was a million miles away from some of the holes I'd stayed in on the road. Guess that was what you got when you were Stanley Cup wannabes.

Management hustled us to a private dining room and shut the door, and we sat down. I noticed how the D-men sat together, the forwards as well, and then the two goalies—Stan and his backup, who apparently was moving on at the end of this season if you believed the rumors—had a table all to themselves.

We ordered food, and the door opened and I expected something other than what arrived. A short woman, age undetermined, holding on to a skinny guy's arm, came into the room. Dressed from head to toe in orange—Flyers orange—she was so damn bright in the sea of men in suits.

"We win!" she cackled and flung her arms wide. I saw the skinny man slink to one side, then realized who it was. The figure skater Trent Hanson, the one who'd done the reality show with the Railers the summer before. He sidled off to sit at the table where Dieter was holding a seat for him.

Right, so Dieter's boyfriend's nana was a Flyers fan.

Unfortunate.

"You all garbage," she added, and looked around for a seat. I saw everyone, to a man, slink down in their seats, but they were lucky—they didn't have space. Our table did, and I heard Westy curse to my side.

Bright Orange Woman came to our table and sat down opposite me. I'd done my season as a Flyer, I'd worn the orange, and she leveled her best stare at me.

"Lola," she announced. I guessed that was her name. "You should never have left the Flyers."

It wasn't as if I'd had a lot of choice; I was a journeyman, sent to whatever team needed a grinder like me.

"I like it here," I said defensively.

She huffed and narrowed her eyes. "You're dangerous to my Flyers."

I wasn't going to disagree with that. I knew my worth.

Then she held court. She was outrageously opinionated, rude, vocal in her dislike of the Railers, and I loved her. She was so damn funny, and by the end of the night we had our heads together talking about the glory days of hockey, of which she had seen way more than me. I loved hockey. I could quote stats, team logos, recall that time when Mario did something to

Wayne or Clarke deked Favell. I was a walking ency-clopedia of crap about hockey.

Halfway through a tirade from Lola about Ten being too fast and how it just wasn't fair to all the other teams, it hit me with the force of a ton of bricks.

What would I do without hockey? Who was I without the knowledge of the game?

What will happen to me?

Grief curled in my chest and stayed there for the remainder of dinner, and if anyone noticed how quiet I had got, they didn't say.

Lola hugged me and patted my cheek—the one on my face—then she pressed a kiss to my hand. She didn't actually say anything, but I was unaccountably moved by it all. All of a sudden, I wanted her to hold me while I cried.

Where the hell had that come from?

Then the fear hit. Was I sad because I was leaving hockey? Or was it because the thing in my brain was changing the way I saw things? I was the hard guy, not the one who cried. Was something wrong?

I headed for my room, damn pleased I didn't have to share—thank God, they'd stopped that shit—and stripped off my suit, taking care to hang it up. I made the call, sitting there in my underwear in the warm room, hoping to hell the doc would pick up. I paid him enough to be on call for me, surely.

I got an answering service, but they connected me

quickly, and within five minutes of getting the thought of dying right front and center in my head I was talking to the only man who could calm me down.

"What's wrong?"

Doctor Nolan Warner was a field expert in endovascular neurosurgery. He'd spent some time rooting around in my brain nearly seven years ago, and I had him on speed dial. I couldn't recall the last time I'd spoken to him. I ignored headaches and dizziness of any kind; I'd decided I'd rather not know a long time ago.

But this was different. This was my last year, and I didn't want to die before I finished. I had a job to do, a Cup to lift.

"Max, hello," he said, all conversational and happy.

"I have a headache," I blurted out.

There was silence. He'd explained the things to look out for—extreme headaches, dizziness, blurred vision, sickness, memory loss. I didn't have any of those.

"On a scale of one to ten—"

"It's a one," I admitted.

Of course to a normal guy that might have been a five, but to a hockey player, pain at the level of one was nothing. Skaters our there played with broken legs —a level one headache was nothing.

He didn't sigh or call me an idiot for contacting

49

him. The line was quiet for a moment and then I heard him move and close a door.

Had I woken him up? What time was it in Vancouver anyway?

"Talk to me," he said in that soft, insistent, doctor-like tone.

"When you blocked it, you told me there was a chance it could come back."

"No, I told you the work I had done on your particular arteriovenous malformation led me to believe there was a ninety percent chance you wouldn't experience any further issues."

"With that site," I insisted.

Doc had explained that even though the tangle of blood vessels in my brain had been capped and blocked like a new oil well, there was a slim chance the issue would always be there. Ten percent that it would worsen if I persisted in carrying on with any kind of contact sport.

Ten percent I could handle. Hell, I was more likely to get hit by a bus than have any of his intricate work in my brain fail. I didn't drive anymore—I wasn't ready to be a loaded weapon on the freeway— and my will was up-to-date, with everything I had going to my sisters.

But.

Seven years, headaches, and I was so close to the end of my career.

"Tell me again about the possibility of secondary

sites," I said. When they fixed one site, that could mean the pressure backed up elsewhere. The percentage chance was small, but there, nevertheless. Hence me not driving.

He didn't. Instead, this time he sighed. "When will you be in Vancouver?"

"I'm not," I began. After all, we didn't know how far we would go in the final, let alone if the Canucks would, or even if they would meet us at any point.

"Max, I meant book a time to see me in Vancouver. I'll run some tests."

I held on to the words. He wanted to run some tests. *He thinks something is wrong.* My stomach churned, my chest tightened, and I felt hot and vulnerable and shaky all at once.

"You said I had to be careful," I blurted. The poor guy had a miserable son of a bitch whining down the phone at him. What the hell was wrong with me?

"Max, calm down."

I did. Immediately. Like Pavlov's dogs and the bell, I reacted to the stern, unforgiving command and the tension uncoiled inside me.

"Book an appointment with my service. Or don't. Maybe just fly up and pay me a visit when you can. Or don't. Either way, come to see me. But worrying about a level one headache isn't practical, and I'm concerned there's an underlying psychological issue here."

That was so not what I wanted to hear. My brain was perfectly fine, thank you very much.

Well, except for the AVM, the risk of death, and the fact I was losing my shit.

I said goodbye, told the doc I would visit, and hung up.

The room was utterly quiet apart from my breathing, not even the sound of the street twenty stories below. And I felt aimless. I should sleep, but the loss of the game and the morose thoughts that balled in my chest kept me tossing and turning in bed. In the end I got up, retrieved my iPad, and sat on the sofa in the corner of the room with a hot chocolate. I checked the news, took one look at the shitty headlines and shut that down. I opened Candy Crush, but the colors were too bright and I wasn't concentrating.

Something about the game I was playing reminded me of Ben.

Who was I kidding? As soon as I stopped doing anything concerning hockey, it was Ben that filled the void.

Just as I've played with a lot of teams, I've been with a lot of men, all kinds of men. But Ben was different.

I just couldn't figure out what it was that made him different.

Maybe it was because I was sitting there in the dark staring at a game with candy and thinking about a fuck in a car with a sexy, sleek, dark-skinned Adonis.

Maybe it was because he was a tall drink and I was thirsty. Maybe he was shiny-new, and I'd eventually fuck him out of my system.

I recalled the noises he made—the sighs, the gasps —the fact he took me inside him and screwed back onto me and wanted more. And the kisses.

I was getting hard, and I savored that delicious expectation of getting myself off to the sounds he made and to the sensation of fucking up into him.

But first I wanted to see his photo, find out more, and I recalled he ran a no-kill shelter. Last Roads? Dog Roads? Or something Roads. I googled no-kill shelters in Harrisburg, and there it was, first on the list: Crossroads No-Kill.

His picture wasn't on the front page; that honor belonged to Diana Pierce, who held the title of Kennel Manager. She was a short, plump woman with curly dark hair, and the picture was of her and an armful of puppies. I did my bit for charity. Maybe I could do something for them, I liked dogs enough to do that. Maybe I could set up something in my will that would send some cash to the shelter. Hell, being a grinder didn't pay like the superstars, but at one time I'd been pulling in two mill a season, not to be sniffed at.

I clicked through the pages, adoption histories, testimonials, things about the visiting vet Dr. Vince Owens, and I read up on the adoption counselor, Abby, who had written a post about how dogs impact lives. The website was professional, informative, but I still hadn't found what I was looking for.

And then there it was. A stunning photo of Ben and his dog who looked like a husky, although the description called it a malamute, and a short paragraph about why he'd taken over the shelter. I hardened even more and palmed my cock; what I wouldn't give to have him under me right here and now. Or bent over the desk in the corner, or on his knees.

I don't know what I clicked, but suddenly there was a new picture on my screen, of Ben and another man. They weren't hugging or holding hands, but Ben was looking at him, and the depth of love in his eyes was plain to see.

I read the article, and my erection went away faster than Ten on a breakaway.

That was Liam, Ben's husband, who'd died young, quickly, tragically, but who inspired Ben on a daily basis to continue the battle for rehousing dogs. He was blond, with bright blue eyes, and the pup in his arm was a tiny version of the one in the photo of Ben alone. The label underneath said, "Liam, Ben, and Bucky". I wondered what he'd died of, and then I saw the charity link for *multiple myeloma*, which upon further reading I learned was aggressive and fast.

I'd played the what-if game so many times. When they told me what was wrong with me, I'd asked them would it be quick, or slow. They'd had no answer. Would I prefer to go quickly, or to linger for a long time? If it was slow, then I'd have time to say goodbye to everyone. My mom, my sisters, the friends I'd made during my time in hockey. I had people who would miss me.

Just not the one person, a man who loved me as much as Ben had obviously loved his husband, Liam.

I went to bed after that. The idea of getting off had gone, the need for it dwindled to nothing.

We'd lost a game. Ben had lost a husband. I was close to losing everything.

Who the hell could sleep after all that?

WE WON THE NEXT GAME. I don't know how it happened, but if we could bottle the energy we had in that game, we'd be rich. Ten was the first to bury the puck in the net on a power play. The other team's defense was sloppy, tired…who knows? All I knew for sure was they were letting us through.

Maybe Ten was faster?

Maybe Connor was trickier?

Maybe the Railers' D-men were just that good?

Or maybe it was Stan, who did some inhuman tending, at one point literally doing a cartwheel to grab a puck out of the air when it rebounded off the post.

A shutout.

A three to nothing win for us, and the series was

tied at one all, ready for the home games back in Harrisburg.

The mood in the locker room was lighter, and I wondered what Coach would do this time. His tone was happier but his message was the same.

"You played well. I saw really good things on the ice. Well done."

This time, though, Mads came around and high-fived his D-men, and I couldn't help smiling. Even if my thigh did hurt like a bitch from taking a puck in front of the net. Even with padding, a hundred-mile-an-hour projectile leaves a mark.

"Get it seen to," Mads insisted, and pointed at my thigh. "Back to the plane in two hours, but I want to see that iced and fixed."

There was nothing that could truly *fix* the bruise I'd have, but we could at least attempt to lessen it. Ten was in the room with me—he'd taken a pretty shit hit into the board on a power play when I'd been on the bench gassed after my shift. They'd kept him on, and he'd been a fucking target. Poor kid.

"This is just the start," I said to him when he grimaced at the ice and poked at his arm.

"Fucker slashed me," Ten muttered, and tested his hand, opening and closing the fist. He'd bounce back. I remembered being his age, ready to conquer the world and find my place.

"Look after yourself," I replied. Then wished I

hadn't said a word at all, because Ten got that look in his eye.

"You sound off," he observed. "We won."

"A win doesn't always mean you get to smile all the way home." I realized I sounded like an idiot, like some kind of fake Mr. Miyagi, and Ten called me on it in the best way. He snorted a laugh, and then the laugh became something more, and then he couldn't stop laughing, and pretty soon I was joining in.

"Wise words say you," he managed between laughs. "Do, there is no try." That last one had him near wetting himself, I swear, and I couldn't help but feel lighter around him.

By the time we left the therapy room, we were chuckling and exchanging stupid one-liners from films. Turned out for a young guy he knew a lot of old films.

I told him so, and he looked at me as if I was an idiot.

"Max van Hellren, six two, two-thirty pounds, defense, shoots right, selected sixty-first overall in the oh five draft, aged thirty. Right?"

"You memorized all that shit?"

"Yep," Ten said cheerfully. "Mads kept going on and on about wanting you, and he wouldn't let it rest. My point here is you are not that much older than me. What is with you guys and your obsession with age?" He laughed again as I swatted at him and he ducked.

"Too slow, old man," he said, then jogged away. I could have jogged after him, but I was tired, and I rolled my neck and followed at a more sedate pace.

The flight back was quiet. We had two days until our next game with Philly, at home, and aside from practice and sleep, there was one other thing I wanted to do.

See Ben.

HOW I WAITED that long I didn't know. After practice I caught a cab the short distance from my big empty apartment to the shelter, the words of the coach playing in my head.

He wanted us to watch out for Ten. Protect Ten. And not just Ten, but the others who held our best chances against this strong team. That was what I was concentrating on when the cab delivered me to the gates of Crossroads No-Kill Shelter. There was a buzzer, and I pressed it.

"Hello, can I help?" a female voice asked me.

"I'm here to see Ben," I said. Because that was fact.

"Could I have your name, sir?"

"Max."

There was a moment when I thought she'd ask more, but this was a shelter open to visitors, right? So, they'd let people in. Including a horny hockey player.

I patiently waited, and Diana, the smiling brunette from the website, bounded up to me.

"I'm sorry, sir, the shelter isn't open until three for viewings today, and Ben is out back with some new arrivals. Can I help? Are you looking to adopt?"

I could lie here, tell her I was there for a dog, but I couldn't give a pet a home now. It would just have to be rehomed if anything happened to me.

"No, this is a personal visit."

She blinked at me—clearly that was a new one to her—and then she looked indecisive, her eyes glancing right, to where I assume Ben was working. I could just walk over and find him, but that was going to get her all worked up about security, I could tell. I interrupted her train of thought.

"Can you tell Ben that Max the hockey player is here for him?"

She nodded and turned to leave, but she didn't need to.

"It's okay," Ben called from a path to the right of us. "Come on over, Max."

I grinned at Diana, and we parted with her looking a lot less worried.

He shook my hand. "Sorry about that. The vandalism has us all on edge."

I wondered what itty-bitty Diana would do against a big guy like me. I thought maybe they needed to up their security and not let idiot hockey players in through the gate. I didn't say that, though. I was too busy holding Ben's hand and not letting go even when he tugged his away.

For a moment we stood there, and he tilted his head a little in thought.

"It took you a bit of time to find me," he said, with a soft and secretive smile.

"Sorry, I had some hockey to play." I released his hand, and he stepped back and away.

"Want to see some puppies?"

I was hoping that was a euphemism for sex, but no, he really wanted me to see puppies, seven of them, fat black lab puppies in a writhing group of noisy yaps and jumps. I didn't know why they were there or what their story was, but I was lost, and fuck me if I wasn't ready to take them all home. Right then. In the passenger seat of a cab, and the back seat, and anywhere they wanted to sit.

When I looked at Ben, he grinned at me, and shit, I was lost.

Because that smile was powerful stuff.

Chapter Five

Ben

W hat amazing eyes the man had.

That was what was pounding around my head as I scooped up a wriggling black ball of fur and handed it to Max. His were brownish-gold. Stunning, really. Always hot. Like a low-banked wood stove. I enjoyed looking at his eyes. Hell, I enjoyed looking at his everything. I'd always been a sucker for jocks. Liam had been one hell of a tennis player and had even entertained thoughts of going pro, but elbow issues during college had stalled those plans.

Hey, dipshit. Stop thinking about Liam. Focus on this man here. The living, breathing one with the killer smile and incredible arms.

"You like dogs?"

Max nodded, allowing the pup to slather his face

with kisses reeking of puppy breath. "Oh yeah, love them."

That was a large tick in a massive box.

"Cats?"

"Sure."

Another box checked.

Now I had nothing. Shit. I looked around the back of the kennels, eager to find anything to talk about. Max was enjoying his face-washing, so the awkward silence dropping over us like a cloak wasn't noticed by him as much.

Two kids on bikes pedaled past. "When I was ten, I took a header over my handlebars. Had to get ten stitches right here."

I pointed under my chin. Max reached out and tipped up my chin with two beefy fingers.

Then he kissed the scar. Lust flared to life low in my stomach, the heat creeping out to warm my extremities, which included my dick.

"Uh, okay." I just stood there, puppies bouncing over my shoes, and allowed the man to place a few more kisses to my throat, the one on my Adam's apple sliding into more sucking than kissing. My cock thought the sucking was mighty fine.

"When do you get off?" he asked, voice as rough as sandpaper.

"As soon as we find somewhere to be alone."

That made Max chuckle and me blush. I'm usually not that forward with men. It had taken me weeks to fumble-bumble around Liam, making a fool of myself, until he took pity on me and asked me out.

"I didn't mean that." He released my chin, and our gazes met. One eyebrow crept up his brow. "Obviously, I did mean it, but it wasn't supposed to come out. You make me sloppy."

"How about we get something to eat, talk a bit, and then go find somewhere to get you off?" He placed the pup down with its litter-mates.

"I need to finish getting these guys into the shelter files."

"I can wait." He moved back a few inches, which was a relief. Sort of. "Why are they here?"

I dashed off some notes on my iPad. "They were dumped under the Market Street Bridge."

His eyes rounded. "Like tossed into the river in a bag?"

"No, thankfully. Just left by the water in a box." I might have raised a lip.

"Fucking people suck."

"That they do." I lifted my attention from the admission information. "We'll gather them up and put them in an isolated part of the shelter for new arrivals. Tomorrow our vet will come out and check them over, give them shots, worm them."

"And then you can help them find homes."

I smiled. "Fingers crossed. Puppies go fast. It's the old dogs that no one wants."

He seemed to drift for a moment, perhaps

thinking back to an old canine friend he might have had. Then, just as fast as he'd left, he was back. Eyes snapping to me, that familiar fire kindled in the depths of amber and brown.

"Sorry, I was somewhere else."

I waved off his concern, and we toted the puppies into solitary, which was a stretch of kennels that were separate from the main runs. No outside areas, since we didn't know whether incoming dogs were safe for human interaction. The pups rolled over each other, glad for the bowls of chow and water Diana had set out for them. She stood off to the side, her mouth twitching, her eyes moving from me to Max as he and I talked about the pups.

Then he turned to Diana. "Think I can steal him away?"

"I think so." She gave me the sauciest wink, then padded off.

"So, food. Did you eat lunch?"

"Ah, no, not yet. I meant to, but I was up to my ears in paperwork. Coming out to admit the pups is really Diana's job, but I begged to do it. Being cooped up works on me after a few hours."

"I get that." He stepped around me and pulled open the door leading to the offices and medical room.

"Let me just get Bucky and we can go."

"Bringing your dog?"

"I can't leave him behind." I tugged open my

door and Bucky trotted out, tail wagging, eager to greet Max again. The big man ruffled his gray fur with a large hand between the ears.

"Going to be hard to find a place to eat with a dog," he pointed out.

"Just leave that to me."

An hour later we were strolling along the paths at Wildwood Lake, a wonderful park that featured wetlands, bike and running paths, and was dog friendly as long as your pooch was leashed. Max and I sat on a bench in the shade of a hundred lush trees, just off a running path, eating some hoagies we'd picked up as Bucky sat at attention, on the watch for squirrels.

I learned a lot about the man I'd been so intimate with. We both talked about our childhoods, our plans for the future, and our shared love of sports. He told me a couple of humorous stories about old girlfriends and boyfriends, which answered that big question as well.

Our tastes in music were sort of similar, although he confessed he wasn't big into music. We liked the same movies and watched a few of the same shows on TV. He wasn't much of a reader anymore, he admitted, but did enjoy thrillers. I had a weakness for all things Stephen King even though they scared the wits out of me. Max smiled easily, laughed even more easily, and touched me in soft, private ways he didn't seem ashamed of.

After a small brush of his fingers over my forearm, I leaned over to press my lips to his. He never shrank back or acted afraid of being seen kissing a man.

"You ready to go get naked?" he asked, his words dancing over my lips.

"Yeah." I had been dreaming about this big man spread over my bed, thick legs and strong arms akimbo, offering all that hairy burly man to me to do with as I wished.

We made the drive to my place. Feeling guilty as all hell, I called the shelter just to make sure my staff was okay with me stealing a couple of hours. This had never happened. Ever. I threw a peek sideways, caught sight of Max and my skin flushed. That man had some kind of wild effect on me.

I noticed the parking space for my aunts was empty and thanked God and all the angels that my aunts were off picketing some poor senator or congressman or judge today. Yes, they still drove. No one at the DMV *dared* to take their driver's licenses away.

Once inside my tall, skinny house, I nervously went around opening the windows as Max meandered about, looking at the well-worn furnishings.

"Nice house. Homey. This your husband?" He lifted a picture of Liam and me back in college, both soaked from a tumble from our canoe on a trip we'd taken one spring along the Tioga River in upstate Pennsylvania.

"Yeah, that's Liam."

Now I felt icky. Like I was cheating on Liam somehow by bringing Max to our house.

"Do you still want this?"

My gaze snapped from the old cork coasters on the coffee table. Liam had bought those when we'd gone to New York City for a Yankees game four years ago.

"I do, yeah." I offered him my hand. His abrasive palm slipped over my damp one. I led him upstairs to one of two bedrooms—mine, the largest. A soft summer breeze wafted in when I threw the window open. The sounds of the neighborhood drifted in. Kids playing, the steady drone of traffic, someone shouting, the wail of a far-off siren. City noises. Max pulled his shirt over his head. I reached behind me to place my wedding picture face down.

God, but he was a lot of man. Wide where he should be, lean where it counted. I stood riveted to the carpet, my ass resting on the dresser, as he nonchalantly peeled off all his clothes while his gaze and mine remained tangled.

"Looking a little rough in the daylight, huh?"

I shook my head. "Not at all." Yeah, he had some scars. Didn't we all? Nothing that turned me off. Far from it. All those nicks and dents from life added to his appeal, just like the small wrinkles by his amazing eyes.

He made his way across to me, long-legged

masculinity and cocky walk, my cock plumping up more with each step closer.

"You are so beautiful," he said, his hands sliding up under my shirt, pushing the collar to my chin and then tugging my shirt over and off my head. I reached for his cock, slid my fingers around it, down to the base and then back up, palming the smooth head.

Time slowed, or it seemed to. His mouth slanted over mine, his fingers plucking at my nipples as I stroked him. Then time sped up, tossing me into the bed with Max under me, my pants lying over the dresser, his cock weeping, streaking my cheek with salty precum as I rubbed my face against his prick.

We rolled and grappled, teasing with touch and tongue, laughing lightly at his knee popping or his shoulder creaking when I raised his arms over his head and nibbled my way over his biceps to the thick mat of underarm hair and then down his ribs.

"I want to fuck you," I panted against his navel. He arched up. I speared the small indent, and he groaned. It was a thrilling sound, at least to me. Rasping and breathy, it went right to my balls, making them feel heavier.

"Yeah, fuck me, Ben."

I slithered up over him, sweaty chest gliding over sweaty chest, and fumbled around in the drawer of the nightstand. There were no condoms, only lube.

"You got any protection?" I asked. He nodded.

"Wallet."

A moment later I was back in bed, easing his knees up to his chest and then booting up, his tight hole on display for me. My hands were shaking so badly that rolling the condom on was tricky. I got a bit too much lube on my fingers, but he didn't seem to care when it trickled down the crack of his ass. I guess my fingers slipping in and out of him kind of made a damp spot on my covers inconsequential.

"Get in me, Ben. And do not play around with being gentle. I can take what you got and then some."

I threw him a defiant look. He gave me a quirky smirk. "Okay, so this is a dare is it? Like my dick can't fuck you hard enough to make you speak in tongues?"

I took my cock in hand and patted his slick opening.

"Take it as you want, gorgeous."

So I did. I took it just as I wanted. Thrusting into him, going as deeply as I could. Max growled in pleasure, his fingers tightening on his knees. I pushed in deeper yet, grinding my pelvis in small circles, eager to hear him make that snarling, passionate sound again. I got it. And that made me feel like a king. Pulling out, I went deep once more, and was rewarded with another guttural groan.

"Do that until I come all over myself. No going slower. Fuck me, Ben. Make me know I'm alive."

I lifted my gaze from where we were joined. His amber eyes were ripe with emotions I couldn't place. Lust for sure, but something else. Sadness? Fear?

He clamped down on me, squeezing my cock with his inner muscles, and I stopped worrying about much of anything. My focus fell to the rhythm, the speed, the pull of his body on mine as I pumped in and out of all that tight, hot man.

"Shit. Ah shit, shit, shit," I huffed when I felt the surge of an impending orgasm sparking to life. Max lay under me, slick with sweat, pumping his fat cock in perfect time with my thrusts. And just like that I blew apart. Using my knees for purchase, I wiggled up even further, mad to bury myself in him far and hard. He grunted long and low and came on his chest and stomach. A few pearly drops landed on his chin. Even gripped in the madness of a world-class release, I dropped over him, losing some depth but gaining the rich, heady taste of his cum on my tongue. I lapped at the hair on his chin, then dove into his mouth, tongue slipping over his.

"Oh shit," I said yet again when the kiss broke.

Max slung a big arm over my lower back, then stretched his legs out, grimacing slightly. He rolled us over, tacky cum sealing our chests, and plundered my mouth as if he'd never kiss a man again. I clung to him like a climbing rose, wanting nothing more than to keep this fiery intimacy going. But it couldn't linger forever. Life had to ease back into our little afternoon delight. I snorted at myself for even thinking of that song at this moment. I touched his face with my fingertips, smoothing out the lines on his forehead as I began humming that silly song.

"Oh Christ," Max chortled, falling to lie beside me as a warm summer wind worked on drying our skin. "You're an idiot."

That made me laugh out loud. "This is the kind of lunch break I need every day."

"Tell me about it." He rolled to his back and stared at the ceiling. "Morning skate, food, sex with a hot man, and a nap. Perfection."

I snorted, then had to leave the bed, and the sexy man, to take care of the condom. I pattered out to the hall, then ducked into the lone bathroom. When I came back, Max was pulling his jeans up over his ass. Seeing that made me a little sad. I'd been hoping to steal a little more time with him.

His sexy gaze touched mine. "You think you might want to come to the next game?" That made me feel a little better. "I mean, I know we're not freaking *Washington* or anything."

He couldn't hide his smile. Neither could I.

Which was how I found myself wedged between a glittery figure skater in makeup wearing a funky green hat with feathers, and a round little Asian woman in an orange Flyers sweatshirt at the next game.

"Ah! You see that?! That dirty pool! What you look at?"

I quickly averted my gaze from the irate woman shaking a fist at Max for leveling one of the Flyers.

"*Lola*, stop pestering Benton."

I tried to look back at the other women around us —who I assumed were wives and girlfriends—but the long pheasant feather on Trent's hat poked me in the eye.

"Oops! Sorry. Damn my feathers." Trent handed me a lime green handkerchief to dab at my watering eye. "So, dish. Tell me how you and Max became an item."

"Oh, well, uh…we're not really an item. Just friends." As if I was going to discuss Max and me with a man I'd just met thirty minutes ago.

"Mmm-hmm. Friends with benefits. *Lola*, what did I tell you about making that gesture at the Railers?"

"I flip off Rowe. He make bad move on my man!" The tiny woman held both middle fingers way over her head.

Trent sighed. "She never listens." I'd never seen a more flamboyantly out man in my life, and I was thirty. "Right, so back to you and Max."

"There is no me and Max," I said once again, nearly missing an amazing shot on goal the Flyers goalie barely managed to block. Man, Tennant Rowe was fast. If this team faced Washington in the next round, it was going to be bedlam around the goal of my beloved team.

"Oh yes, right. There *is* no you and Max. I wonder why he forked up the cash for these special seats if he's not diddling you—or you're not diddling him—in the derrière. *Lola!* I mean it, you stop doing that with your mouth right now! There are children nearby!"

The pudgy woman in bright orange sat down, muttering in her native tongue. I didn't want to know what she'd been doing with her mouth.

"Listen, Trent, I know this is going to sound rude, but can we not talk about what Max and I are doing in bed and just watch hockey?" I waved my tissue at the men on the ice.

"Ah! So you and Max *are* diddling each other in the derrière! I knew it! I have a sixth sense for gay naughtiness. I want details. He's a big, bad boy in bed, I bet."

I gaped at the man in green and yellow. "No. I'm not sharing details."

"Spoilsport," Trent said, then laughed lightly. I suspected the man would have all the dirt on Max and me before the night was over.

Midway through the game, my phone vibrated. I pulled it out of the pocket inside my sweater and saw it was Diana calling. Which was odd. She rarely called unless it was an emergency.

"Give me a few," I yelled into my phone. Diana might have said "okay" but it was hard to say as the crowd was booing a bad call against the Railers.

"Let me know what happens," I shouted near Trent's ear. "I have to take this call."

He nodded. I stepped around feet and cups of

beer until I was out of our aisle, then I jogged up the stairs and ducked into the nearest men's room.

"Okay, what's wrong?" We'd dealt with increasing vandalism the past few weeks. Busted glass in the front door, people trying to jimmy the locks on the windows, and a rather nasty racial slur painted on the side of the building a few days ago.

"I just got a call from the manager of Secure-Guard Security to confirm we'd be at the shelter tomorrow at eight to allow his technicians in. Did you order this and forget to tell me?"

I slipped around two men washing their hands and stepped into a stall. "No, no way. There's not enough petty cash in the till to cover new chew toys, let alone installation of a security system. Did you tell them it was a mistake?"

"I did, but they stated the work order had been verified and the total had been paid for. In cash."

"In cash?" I shifted my foot a bit to avoid a small puddle on the floor. "Who the hell has money like that lying around? And who would spend it on us?"

"I have no idea. I told him I'd call him back. What should I say?"

Someone flushed a urinal. "Did they say who paid for it?"

"An anonymous dog lover."

"What the shit?"

"Right?! Do you really think we have some rich,

secret benefactor now? It would be incredible if we did."

"I honestly don't know what to think." Male conversation floated into the stall. I pondered for a long moment. "Okay, well, let's call them back and tell them to go ahead, then. Looks like God has decided to smile on us for a change."

I exited the stall and walked out into the arena while Diana yelped in glee. The crowd was clapping. I checked out the replay on the Jumbotron and was treated to the sight of Max knocking a Flyers defenseman over the boards into the Railers bench. A totally clean hit, but brutal and clearly delivered to send a message. I smiled at the replay and the gleam clear in Max's eyes. Yep, God sure was smiling on us of late.

Chapter Six

Max

Winning the next three games meant the Flyers were out of the race and we advanced to the next round. I patted Lola's shoulder when I saw her after the game. She looked devastated, and not even Ten reassuring her that the Flyers were a "really good team" seemed to help. I remembered what it was like to be a fan who loved a team as passionately as she did and had to watch their team lose.

We weren't sure who we'd be facing at this point —the two other teams in our bracket still had a game to go—but in a way, I hoped it was Washington. Mostly so I could get tickets for a game where Ben could see the team he loved. Of course, I didn't really want us to end up playing the team from a hockey point of view; they were a hard team to beat. I didn't have to read pundit summaries to know that even though we'd finished ahead of them in the points, that they'd been strong recently, and the Railers would be the underdog in that match.

But there was also a small part of me that wanted to show Ben what I was made of; that I was good enough to play on a team that could beat the one he loved.

And how ridiculous was that? Masculine posturing at its worst.

Why did I feel I had to impress Ben? We'd only managed one more get-together but it had started well enough. The sex had been explosive, amazing. When we'd laid back on the bed, we'd so nearly cuddled, I swear it. But his phone had rung. Someone had thrown a brick through a window at the shelter, and he'd had to leave because Diana was on a training course and there was no one else who could deal with it all.

Fuck.

That cuddle had been *so* close.

I loved cuddles. Not the hugs you got when your team scored, those quick bro-hugs that gave you a face of sweat and ice, but real hugs. Not a lot of people held me, but then I *was* edging on the wrong side of scary.

I even scared my mom. Or at least I think I did.

My PTA-mom. Loved ballet recitals with my two

little sisters, threw girlie parties, had a lot of pink in her house. She just never quite knew what to do with her big, tough son. Maybe if Dad had been around it would have been different, but he'd moved on when I was little and died three years ago in a work-related accident.

She supported my hockey but didn't quite understand it. She loved that I earned big money, that I had a name, but she hated I beat on other teams for a living. I was, to her, a mass of contradictions.

Mom and my sisters had been in the stands for our last game and she'd been so pleased when we'd met up afterward, but she hadn't hugged me.

Nor had she hugged Ben, whom I'd introduced as a friend, with a lot of emphasis on the word *friend*.

That was another thing that didn't sit quite right with my mom. She'd never caused a scene when I'd chosen to bring a guy home, but I could see the confusion in her eyes every time I did. She'd loved my junior high school girlfriend, Jenna. And Abby, whom I'd been dating when I was drafted. However, she hadn't gelled with Dan, or Eric. There was no way in hell she'd gel with Ben.

Not only that, but they knew nothing about my brain thing. What was the point? They'd start telling me it was all hockey's fault even if wasn't. I'd been born with it, so even though it wasn't a hereditary thing, I could still point at my mom and tell her it was her or Dad's fault.

Even if it wasn't, and even if I would never say something like that.

I might not get on with my mom, but she was still my family. Right?

So yeah, I was one big bundle of mess where my family was concerned, and the night before I'd wanted a damn hug.

I sent a quick text to Ben asking him if he was okay, and about the shelter, then a separate text to the salesman at SecureGuard who'd assured me his damn system would stop all this petty shit.

He called me back immediately, all contrite and explaining they would be out as soon as they could to expand the something of the whatever. To be honest, I wasn't really listening much past the part where they promised to up their game and protect the shelter. I ended the conversation with a gentle reminder I was an anonymous donor and waited for the assurance that it would stay that way.

Then I focused back on today, on packing my stuff for a two-game road trip in Washington. I ended up on the plane next to Adler, who had his cap pulled down over his face and looked to be asleep. Seemed like maybe our marketing guy had been keeping him up in more ways than one.

"It's not good for you," I pointed out helpfully when I saw him peeking at me as I belted in.

"What?" he yawned widely.

"Sexual relations the night before a big game."

"Actually, I couldn't sleep—had a whole head of nightmares about bright orange penguins pecking out my eye." He shuddered. "And hell, did you just use the term 'sexual relations'?" He smirked, and I flicked at his cap.

"Get some sleep asshole," I added with the authority of being older and wiser than Adler Lockhart.

"You're just jealous of me and Layton," he murmured, and settled back in his seat.

Jealous? What did I have to be jealous about? Yeah, Adler and Layton were into each other in a big way, but I had some of my own.

I sort of had Ben.

Ben, who was, *I-think-could-be* more than a hookup, but of course way less than a boyfriend. A friend with benefits, where benefits were confined to fucking.

Sadly not including post-fuck cuddling.

"Look!" Stan hovered next to me and thrust something in my face, and abruptly I had a lap full of drawings. "Help make choice," he ordered.

I realized you didn't argue with Stan. Not because he was intimidating, but because once you went down the rabbit hole of trying to understand what he was saying, it was ten minutes you'd never get back.

I looked at the sketches, clearly for a helmet design, and they were gorgeous. There was the Railers logo—the old steam engine, with steam curling around the sides, and iron and steel crossed.

There was also snow and other things that were, I assumed, Russian.

"Pick," he said.

"You want me to pick one?" I wasn't sure how I'd earned that right, and I wished Adler would come out from under his cap.

"All plane pick one," Stan explained.

Thank God. I wasn't sure I could handle the responsibility of making a monumental decision about a goalie's helmet design. I looked at them again and noticed the sheet held the logo of the designer, the same guy I knew my fellow Railers went to for their tattoo designs. Gatlin Pearce. His stuff was pretty cool, and I made a mental note of his name to contact him about some tattoo ideas of my own.

"I vote this one," I said, and pulled out the most vibrant of the three sketches.

"Good for final," he said. Took the paper and frowned at Adler. He was contemplating waking Adler up, but I shook my head subtly.

I was actually quite happy Adler was asleep—that meant quiet for me—and Stan moved on to Ten, who was in the seat in front of me.

My cell vibrated, and I checked it quickly.

All okay, Ben wrote. *Minimal damage, and dogs are fine. Security guy here on a checkup, which is lucky.*

I hit reply, then contemplated the correct response.

Okay.

That was always a good place to start. I added a smiley face, then backspaced. This was more of a thumbs-up situation, and speaking of thumbs, mine were way too big for the damn tiny phone keys. God knew how I hadn't thrown the thing out of a window before now. It took me so long to write anything at all. This was why emojis were such a good thing. I added the thumbs-up, then considered how to phrase the fact I wished we'd managed a cuddle that morning.

Jesus, if any opposing hockey team could see me now, they wouldn't be fearing the Railers' big bad D-man at all. They'd be laughing.

"D-Man wants a cuddle."

"Look at him, poor Maxxy Waxxy needs a huggy wuggy."

I could imagine the chirping and felt myself go scarlet with embarrassment at the thought of someone seeing that far into my soul. I ended the text with a generic, *see you soon*, and turned off my phone before I could think of the kind of shit I might get if anyone found out about my soft side.

The flight was short, the hotel gorgeous, the views over the city worthy of a picture. Which I didn't send to anyone or share with anyone. Just as my mom didn't completely understand my sexuality, she sure as hell wasn't interested in what city I was in. Which pretty much covered how my sisters felt as well.

Never mind, not like any of that mattered anymore.

I could send a picture to Ben?

Send a picture of a city to a man who is a casual hookup? Yeah, right.

WE LOST one to Washington and won one. God knows how we won anything at all because both games were one penalty after another on both sides. Only Stan in the net was enough for us to have the edge, and we took that win home with us, leading this round three games to their one.

The mood on the plane home was euphoric. If we could win the next games, we could sweep Washington out of the race. The thought of it was enough to have us standing most of the flight, shooting the shit and making so much noise it was a wonder the pilot didn't tell us to shut the hell up.

Only as we neared home did we all quiet down after all, we'd meet the same team in two days on our ice.

I took the time to re-read the message I'd received from Ben, timestamped just after we'd won the second game.

Congrats, was the single word. I kind of wanted more but settled instead for holding that single word close.

I fist-bumped teammates as we disembarked, hugged the bemused flight attendant, laughed, grinned, and got into the cab I'd ordered with one express purpose. To see Ben.

When Ben opened the door to his place, yawning behind his hand, adorably mussed and warm from bed, I stepped in, closed the door, and pulled him into my arms.

He came willingly, all soft and tired, and I held him for so long I knew he would want to know what the hell was going on.

"You won one," he murmured against my throat.

"We did."

"But you're hugging me tight."

"Uh-huh."

"What's wrong?"

"Nothing." I held him even tighter and loved that he let me. "I needed a hug."

He laughed then, a soft sound that I felt run through him. "Happy to help."

We hugged it out, too tired to fuck, content just to snuggle in Ben's huge, soft bed, and we fell asleep in each other's arms.

It was the best win I'd had in a long time, because getting that hug was an even better feeling than beating Washington.

WHAT WOKE ME, I wasn't sure. Maybe it was Ben moving, or the sound of his cell phone, or maybe the urgency of his tone. All I knew was he wasn't in my arms, and when I focused on him in the half-dark, he was getting dressed.

"What time is it?" I tried to focus on my watch to see the time.

"Four," he said, curtly, fearfully, and I was instantly awake.

"What?" I sat upright in bed and pulled off the covers, dressing as fast as him.

"A break-in at the shelter. The cops are there, and they have the guy. I'll drive," he added, and I wasn't going to argue seeing as I didn't have a car there and I didn't really drive anymore.

I followed him out of the house, and we arrived at the shelter in the space of ten minutes to flashing lights and two cops. I was ready to get out of the Jeep and take on whoever had been messing with Ben, but I couldn't do that. I couldn't drop gloves on someone outside the rink. I had to keep my cool.

"It wasn't me!" someone shouted. A kid in a coat stared up at the two cops looking right back at him. He was visibly shivering, despite the coat, and I knew how he felt; it was freaking cold out.

"Shit," Ben cursed, and broke into a jog to get to the cops.

"It's okay, he's okay," he said, and moved between the cops and the boy.

"Sir, the alarm was triggered, and on arrival we found this young man and these." Cop one held up what looked like a pocket knife, and when the light of the street light hit the metal my temper boiled over. Now it was my turn to get involved.

"What the fuck?" I said, all up in the kid's face. He stumbled back and away, and Ben had to catch him and stop him from falling.

"Max, leave it," he said, and his tone didn't leave any room for discussion or disapproval.

"DK? What are you doing?" Ben asked, his hands on the kid's skinny upper arms.

"You said if I needed you I could come, and I tried the key in the gate, and it didn't work so I tried to pick the lock, and I'm cold, Ben, and I needed you."

I listened to the boy, this DK, who seemed to know Ben. Who *needed* Ben.

Ben turned so that DK was behind him and it was him facing the cops. "I'm sorry to waste your time here officers. DK is my nephew."

His nephew? That would explain why I wasn't allowed to pummel him, I guess.

"We'll require a statement," Cop two said, with cop one sighing noisily.

"Tomorrow, okay?" Ben waited. Behind him, the kid was shivering, and I didn't know what the hell to do.

The cops conferred with each other, called the situation in with a string of codes, then drove away.

Which left me, Ben, and DK, standing at the front gate and looking at each other.

"Coffee." Ben said, entering his passcode into the new security keypad and walking inside. As soon as the door closed behind us, all the bravado disappeared from the kid and he slumped in the nearest seat.

"Talk to me, DK," Ben said, and went into a crouch in front of him. I backed away a little and filled the coffee pot, all the time with an ear on what was being talked about.

"Dad went crazy," DK murmured.

"Crazy how?" Ben asked.

"He was... It was..." DK stopped and scrubbed at his eyes, as though he was trying to clear tears.

"We all grieve in different ways," I heard Ben say.

"This isn't Dad grieving, Uncle Ben. This is him losing his job, having no money, and if you heard some of the evil shit he screams at me. Then he..."

Ben placed a hand on DK's knee. "Come on, DK, tell me what happened."

DK looked right at me then, and I was reminded staring wasn't a good thing, so I attempted to busy myself with mugs and coffee, but not before DK showed something to Ben and Ben turned on the full light. Not before I saw the marks.

A vivid scarlet on DK's neck, a purple bloom on his arm, crimson flecks on his wrist.

I heard Ben curse in horror, and I had to physically restrain my anger. Hitting a kid?

What the fuck?

"I won't go back," DK snapped. "You can't make me. I'm eighteen now, and I choose to be with you."

Ben glanced over at me, and there was conflict in his eyes. I wanted him to say that everything would be okay for the kid, that he'd offer him a place to stay. I wanted the man who saved dogs to show the same compassion for his nephew. I needed that as much as I needed a hug, to see purity in someone who was the opposite of me.

"Okay," Ben said, and stood. He held out a hand and pulled DK up and into a hug. "But it has to be above-board. I have to talk to your dad."

DK looked shocked, then shrugged, which looked to me like evidence of self-preservation. Maybe he shrugged off everything in life?

"Dad can't do anything about it. He can't make me go home."

"I know," Ben whispered.

Then DK's tears broke free, and he leaned in to Ben. "Why did Uncle Liam have to die?" he said on a sob.

I watched, frozen on the spot as Ben held his nephew. I swear I saw tears on Ben's face as well, but in this light, I couldn't see for sure.

Why wouldn't a widower cry with his husband's family?

I was a voyeur; the worst kind of watcher, seeing this naked grief I understood but couldn't handle. Instead, I lined up the coffee on the side, took mine, and left the room, following the corridor to where I knew the pups were.

Standing watching them, all curled up together in

a heap of fur, I attempted to find some kind of peace, or understanding, or hell, compassion that I could give Ben with this.

How the hell had this uncomplicated *thing* we had between us become so complex with need and, hell, grief?

I didn't have time for this. I had enough of my own grief banked behind a wall in my head, and I wasn't pulling that out to examine it any time soon.

"I'm taking DK back to my place," Ben said from behind me. I could see his reflection in the glass, and he hovered there, not coming close to me.

"So that's your husband's..." I left it open, waiting for Ben to elaborate, although I hadn't really earned the right to know everything.

"Yeah. My husband, Liam, his brother has three sons. DK is the youngest. Poor kid got caught up in the family reaction when Liam decided to marry me. Then when Liam changed his will and left me everything, the dislike for me turned to hate. Hell, he wasn't even happy for DK to visit, even though DK used to work weekends here as his part-time job."

"But you *are* letting him stay with you now." I needed to know that was real, for the kid with the tears and the bruises.

I'd hurt people worse than the marks I'd seen on DK's skin, but never off the ice. Never in a temper so great I could hurt a kid, or my own son. I hated that doubt about what Ben would do crept into my tone, and I saw my words hurt a little from the way he stiffened.

"He'll always have a place with me." His voice was clipped, and I knew I'd fucked up.

"I didn't mean anything by that. I know you."

He turned to leave, but I swear I heard him mutter that I didn't know him at all.

Great, now I was the one feeling hurt. I caught up with him and grabbed his sleeve, pulled him to a stop, and kissed him, soft and insistent, until, with a sigh, he linked his hands around my neck.

"You don't need to be worrying about this," he said, his dark eyes brimming with emotion.

"I didn't before," I admitted. Honesty was one of my strong points, after all. "But this is a vulnerable young adult, here, and hell, you make it damn hard for me to walk away and not care."

He rested his head on my shoulder, and I heard that sigh again, as if the weight of the world sat on him, heavily. I was a big guy, and I had the space to take some of the worry away from him. It's kind of my thing. Protection. Being the brick wall.

"But you want the worry now? After…what? A couple hookups?"

I tried for lightness in my reply. "I have nothing else to do outside of hockey."

"You're an idiot."

I tapped my head then, "Been hit in the head too many times."

I was joking. It was what any hockey player would say.

But the truth of it was acid inside me.

I did what I do best. I ignored the twist of blood vessels in my brain and carried on.

Chapter Seven

Ben

Harboring DK was making me a nervous wreck. I loved him, and his brothers, but knowing DK's dad, Rolf, was going to roll up at any given time, bubbling with vitriol, had me on edge. He'd never approved of me marrying Liam. He'd boycotted the wedding and taken half the family with him. Of course, he'd turned up at the small reception with its open bar, causing chaos with his prejudiced views. I'd wanted him gone, but the sadness in Liam's eyes had made me hold my tongue.

I hated him, and I didn't have the capacity to hate anyone, so I didn't know where it came from.

Mostly he scared me.

Added to that we had the vandalism, and I'd told the staff at the shelter that no one was to be alone on the premises at any time. We double-checked all locks before leaving for the night.

Home was…well, home was a nest of porcupines.

Glenna and Carol had had to be informed of the situation because Rolf knew where we lived.

My great-aunts had gone off the deep end when they'd seen the bruises on DK's pale skin. It had taken all my persuasive powers to get them not to call the police. Firstly, the cops would likely not send out a patrol car to sit outside our place and protect us. That probably only worked on TV shows and in neighborhoods far more affluent than ours. Secondly, DK—or David Kenneth as Liam liked to teasingly call him, since the kid hated his first name for some reason— was legally an adult. Sure, he could press assault charges, but he refused to do so. And it would be his word against Rolf's, and who would believe a kid with some red on his ledger? Small potatoes. Teen stuff. Tagging old houses, mostly. Stealing a candy bar at a corner store. Same kind of thing that any inner-city kid does—trust me, he could have been doing *much* worse—but DK never could avoid getting caught.

When the offer to attend the fifth game against Washington came from Max, I hesitated.

"Max, I really appreciate these," I said as I gazed at the tickets he'd just placed in my hand, right in the middle of my office.

"*But?*"

"But I'm not sure I should leave the house. What if Rolf shows up?"

Max studied me closely. "Ben, you can't hide the kid in the house forever. And in all honesty, you look like hammered shit."

"Thanks." I scowled, then ran a hand over my face. "I feel like hammered shit."

I hadn't slept well since DK had shown up, and my stomach was an acidic mess. Stress did not sit well on me.

"Come to the game. Bring DK. You need to unwind." He slapped a big hand to the nape of my neck, rubbing and pulling me closer. I let him do both because I really needed a neck rub and the feel of his arms around me. Max was slowly becoming a staple in my life, that thing you awaken and look for, or find yourself reaching for in the night. We hadn't yet even had a true date or spent the night with each other. I longed for those things. Maybe I needed to stop waiting for the things I wanted. God knows life can be short. Horribly short at times. Eyes slipping shut as his fingers worked the hard muscles of my neck, I let the words slip out.

"Bet Washington win."

Max laughed softly. "What kind of bet you have in mind?"

"If they win tonight, you come home with me after the game and spend the night."

The neck rubbing stalled. My breathing stopped as well.

"Hey, I need you to look at me." I opened my eyes and found myself staring into gold-brown eyes that burned with emotion. "Is this something you really want from me?"

"Yeah."

"Can I spend the night if we win?"

The Railers had charbroiled my team the game before. I mean, they'd burned Washington as if they were cheap chicken legs on an open flame.

"You want to?"

"Yeah. I do."

I sucked in a deep breath before I fainted. "Okay then. I'll find an extra toothbrush and put it next to mine."

Max kissed me so hard and for so long, the fainting thing became a worry again.

DK and I were smashed between two of the biggest Railers fans God ever put breath into. Both men looked like linebackers, and they were rabid. Faces painted that smoky blue the Railers jerseys were, bare chests with a steam engine that looked drawn on with a Sharpie, were proudly displayed for all to see. Oh, and they were drunk. Not just pleasantly tipsy, either. I mean drunk off their respective asses. DK thought it was all kinds of funny how the only person in East

River Arena who was cheering the team from Washington was sandwiched between two huge men.

Every time Washington did something good—and that was a lot of times—I cheered and was immediately glowered at. Nothing derogatory had been said yet, but it was just a matter of time, I was sure. Still, I wasn't about to be cowed in front of DK, so I rooted as boldly as a man could root.

"Man, they look like a different team," DK yelled after our big Russian forward took out Tennant Rowe. And I mean he took him *out*. Clean shoulder check that caught Rowe in the chest as he was moving the puck down the boards. The wunderkind went down hard, his shoulder taking the brunt of the impact with the boards. As Rowe lay on the ice, stunned and in some intense pain judging by his face, my team stole the puck and raced at the Railers goalie, the shot from point from our star sailing over Stan's left shoulder and shaking the twine. I leaped to my feet as the red light flared to life.

Mr. Mountain on my right bent down to stare at me, his nose nearly pressed flat to mine.

"You need to…go back home little man." His breath was horrendous. A sickening mixture of stale beer and nacho cheese.

DK leaped to his sneakers. "It's cool. He's dating Max van Hellren."

Okay, then. I guessed Max and I were out. As

soon as he'd said it, DK's face fell as the reality of what he'd spouted sank in.

This was interesting. I had a flash of the upcoming beating I'd get for being black, gay, and a Washington fan.

The face-painted man breathing in my face stared at me dully for a minute. I fisted my fingers in preparation. They might beat me like a rug, but I planned to get at least one punch in before I went down.

Never in a million years did I expect him to scoop me up into a crushing bear hug and kiss me right on the lips.

When my feet were back on the cold cement, I stumbled back into DK, my eyes wide.

"My husband and I love the Heller!" He patted the head of the small man on his left, who smiled and waved around the burly blue-faced fan.

"Oh. Well, cool, then!" I grinned and gave him a thumbs-up, then sat down and tried my best not to get kissed by another man during the rest of the game. I came close again later when Tennant Rowe executed this amazing play right by our blue line. He managed to lift the stick of one of our defenseman and then, in this wild slick move, skipped around him, gathered the puck, and sped at our goalie. He took this blistering shot that somehow went through the four inches of space between our goalie's blocker and the pipe. Mr. Mountain only pounded on my back when Rowe scored, thank the Good Lord.

That goal energized the Railers, but they never could get the next goal needed to tie the game. Washington had won this game and were heading back home.

"Tell the Heller I love him," Mr. Mountain yelled as DK and I moved into the crowd, exiting the arena.

"Will do," I shouted over my shoulder.

It was a beautiful night. Warm and clear, low humidity. DK and I lingered around the players' exit, talking with fans while we waited for the players to emerge.

Max walked out wearing a gray suit that hugged his broad shoulders and meaty thighs perfectly. He was talking with Stan when he saw us. His lips curled into a smile. A rush of affection moved through me seeing him move among the fans, signing caps and programs. He really was a good man. And I really was tumbling for him faster than I should, I knew it. Yet I craved it despite being scared by the knowledge.

"Hello, Benton Dog Man!" Stan clapped me on the shoulder. I winced into a smile. "I am yet looking for good dog. Big one. Long teeths with burning red eyes. You have such dog yet?"

"Ah, no, sorry. No dogs with red eyes, but I'll call as soon as I get one in."

"*Da*. Good. And when call, talk to me only. Not talk with Erik. He wishes friendly dog with curly tail. Pah. I say bad men not scare of happy dog. Bad men scare of wolfhound. You have wolfhound at shelter?"

"No, none of those either. I do have some nice lab mixes. I can have one of the volunteers bring one in for the next Adopt a Pet game break."

Stan mulled that over as Max stepped up beside me, his fingers brushing mine.

"Okay, yes, lab mix is okay good until wolfhound with long teeths come." He nodded, ruffled DK's hair, and went off to find his Erik waiting for him by the players' cars.

"Would it look weird if I kissed the only person in Harrisburg wearing a Washington T-shirt?" Max softly asked as we made our way to our car, which was parked around the front with the rest of the commoners.

"Not sure about that. I think we're already out thanks to someone who shall remain nameless," I teasingly said, giving DK an exaggerated dark look.

"I'm sorry Uncle Ben, I honestly thought that guy was going to pound you into pudding."

I threw an arm around his neck and pulled Liam's nephew in to my side.

"Ah well, not like two guys kissing on this team is anything new," Max stated, then tugged open the door of my car. "I'll meet you at your place in about thirty minutes. I need to run home and pack some stuff."

"Sounds good." I stole a fast kiss, then slid behind the wheel. Max slapped the roof and backed away as we pulled out.

DK and I exchanged glances and he smiled at me.

"Oh, uh, I forgot to tell you I was going to spend the night with Skipper," he said, with no trace that he was lying so he could give me and Max space.

"Oh yeah?" I suspected this was something he was making up, but I ran with it. "You want me to drop you off at his house, then?"

"Yep, yeah, cool." He never looked up from the texts he was sending. Probably to Skipper to inform him he was crashing at his place.

We made the ride to DK's neighborhood, a nice middle-class one, and I followed his direction to Skipper's place.

"You need me to pick you up tomorrow?" I asked as the porch light on the house we'd parked in front of came on. A gangly kid ambled out onto the porch and waved.

"Nah, I'll get Skipper to drop me off. Have a nice night, Uncle Ben."

He ran up to his buddy, exchanged a fist bump, then went inside. The light went off. I raced home, eager to get there before Max and maybe set up something romantic. Or at least change the sheets.

I never did get to change the sheets. Max was waiting for me when I pulled up. I was parking, when my Aunt Glenna toddled out of her row house, slid behind the wheel of her old Lincoln, and pulled away in a cloud of burning oil.

"You come right on in and park quickly, Benton!"

Aunt Carol bellowed. "We see you got an overnight man come to call."

"Lord Almighty, give me strength," I prayed as her shout bounced down the street and into every open window.

"Sorry. I thought I was being discreet," Max said when I ambled up to him, his bag draped over his shoulder. "I even asked the cabbie to douse the headlights so as not to alarm anyone."

"They have ears like a dog," I mumbled before Aunt Carol arrived to give Max a once-over. "Why aren't you old women in bed?"

"We're planning the resistance movement for the weekend. Hmm, hmm, he's a beefy one, Benton." She pinched Max's thick biceps and nodded approvingly. "Always did like my men big and brawny."

"Carol! Stop pinching that man," Aunt Glenna shouted as she waddled down the sidewalk in her robe and slippers. "He's come to pinch Benton!"

"Okay, we're going in now." I pulled Max inside and shut the door on the two old women smiling dirty smiles.

"Your aunts are funny." Max tossed his bag onto the couch, then I moved into his arms.

"Oh yeah, they're hilarious."

I slid my fingers up over his cheeks, enjoying the soft bristles of his beard on my palms. He didn't need to say anything. I was feeling it too. The snap of want mixed with the subtle glow of right. This thing here... this was feeling all *kinds* of right.

"You look like you need kisses." He cupped my ass, yanking me flush to him. "Or do you need something else?"

"You're reading it right. I need kisses *and* I need something else."

The kiss was hot, wet perfection. The something else was even better. Max and I had this top-notch sexual compatibility. We seemed to sense what the other needed or wanted. We found our way upstairs, his bag in tow, and fell into my bed. Bucky circled the bed, whining, anxious about something.

"I'm not hurting him," Max told the dog.

"Let me put him out and then crate him."

I rushed to do both, eager to get back to Max. Bucky ran into his crate in the living room, the same one he'd had since he was a pup. He loved his crate. He felt safe in there. I handed him a dog treat and locked the door, smiling at him as he settled right down after a big pet.

Jogging back up to Max, I was already peeling my shirt off when I hit the bedroom doorway and heard the soft snores.

There he was, spread across my bed, hand on his dick, sound asleep.

I couldn't really be mad at him. Smiling, I threw the lightweight summer blanket over his legs and hips, stripped down to my briefs, and turned off the light.

He was a big man. Heavy, too. Gaining any room to sleep took some nudging and shoving, but I eventually got him over to his side and curled up behind him. The night air rustled the curtains, moving over us, cooling the room, and me. I wriggled closer, fully spooning him , and sighed at the radiant warmth seeping into me. Sleep rolled gently over me.

WHEN I WOKE, it was to the soft song of a robin and warm rays of sunshine. Also, I had a man who weighed the same as a silo lying on me. It was nice, and fluffy, but highly uncomfortable. Still, I lay there for as long as I could, then wriggled out from under him. Max never moved. Didn't sniffle or snuffle or even grunt. The man was a sound sleeper. Probably from all those years spent sleeping in hotel rooms with other guys sawing wood.

I snuck into the bathroom, showered, shaved, and pulled on lounge pants and a tank top. Down to the kitchen I went, eager to get the coffee on and some breakfast ready. Since it was Sunday, I had the day off. Hopefully. Unless we had new intakes arrive. City this big, it was rare not to have a new animal come in every day of the week. I let Bucky out of his crate, then opened the back door for him. He bounded out into the yard. I closed the screen door and let him do his thing in my fenced-in little patch of green.

The windows glowed with sunny warmth as I

moved around my small but homey kitchen. Coffee was soon perking, and I was digging out the makings for some French toast. Music from my phone filled the room, the Miracles' "Love Machine" taking over my body. Pan in one hand, spatula in the other, I broke into a set of fine funky moves. I was a damn fine dancer. Liam always said so.

I spun around, and there stood Max in the doorway, rumpled and freshly out of bed, his arms folded over his chest.

"I cook better with music," I said in reply to his one bushy eyebrow slipping up his brow. "Enjoy the show."

I danced around a bit more, eager to hear him compliment my moves.

"Are you in some sort of pain?" he asked, which kind of stalled my slick steps.

"No, why?"

He shook his head. "You ever watch *Seinfeld*?"

"Sure." I lowered the spatula and frying pan from over my head. I also stopped shaking my ass.

"You kind of look like Elaine when she dances."

My jaw hit my chest. "You think I can't dance?" I was stunned. Liam had always been glowing in his praise of my dancing ability. He'd been so bad in comparison that he'd never fast danced with me because he'd look so bad. Or so he had said.

"Not really, no."

I tossed the frying pan onto the stove. "I can dance."

"No, sorry, you really can't. I mean, that's fine, because I can't either."

I guessed he could sense I was getting mad. "I can dance. You're just not used to seeing such soulful smooth moves."

"If you say so." He pattered to the door and let Bucky in. I was too stunned and hurt to move.

"I can dance."

He walked over to me, took the spatula from my hand, and wrapped me in a huge, warm hug.

"No, you can't." He nuzzled up my neck, nipping and nibbling along my jugular. "Want to go back to bed for a bit?"

"I may never go to bed with you again," I teased. Sort of.

"Now that would be a real pity." He captured my mouth, his breath minty-fresh, then slowly backed me against the still-cold stove. "If I tell you that you dance wonderfully, will you come to bed?"

"Too late for that, *Heller*. I know what you really think." I pushed a hand into his briefs, the backs of my fingers skimming the hard length of him.

"I'll fill your ears with your other talents." Oh, he was smooth. Not as smooth as me on the dance floor, but smooth. "I'll fill your ass with my cock too, if you want."

Oh, yes, I did want. I wanted that *really* badly.

"Benton! You have thirty minutes until morning service. Drop what you're doing and get dressed for church." I cringed at the sound of Aunt Glenna right outside the screen door. Max startled violently. I jerked my hand out of his underwear and cussed.

"You want to watch that talk, Benton. Morning, Max. You're coming to church too." Not a question. A statement.

"Uh, yes ma'am."

"Good boy."

Off she went in her Sunday best.

"I need to move." I sighed and snuggled in close for one more kiss, then we had to get moving, before one of them came back and caught me with my hand around his dick again. I'd ask God to forgive me for groping my man on Sunday morning. I was pretty sure he would. God was cool that way.

Chapter Eight

Max

We only needed one more game to get through to the next round, but Washington weren't taking it easy on us. They'd won game five in our arena, and we were back in Washington for game six. Halfway through this game, we were tied and they were all over Ten like flies on shit. I was currently toe to toe with the big D-man, Vladimir Vleck, six-four, built like a brick outhouse, and his hands in fists in front of him.

I'd already dropped gloves because the asshole had taken Ten into the boards, again, for the second game in a row. Coach wanted me to let it go, work on protecting Ten, but the way they'd had to help Ten off the ice a minute ago had me riled up. Not only that, but the rest of the Railers were suddenly playing with caution, and we couldn't have that.

This game was stale, and it was my role to stir things up.

I waited for Vleck to make the first move. He was chirping some shit about my dick, or my mother, but I wasn't listening. You don't chirp and fight; it makes you sloppy. I saw him drop his shoulder, telegraphing the punch, dodged it, and came out swinging. I got two clean punches in, and he staggered back and gripped my jersey. I buried my skates, leaned into the hold, and he began to lose his balance. I could taste the victory, punching three times more, feeling others pulling at my jersey, hauling me away from the flailing Russian on the ice.

"Fuck you," I said loud enough to hear but hidden enough that I wouldn't get called on it. Toly was between us now, his face split in a wide grin. He patted my shoulder, then went with me and the ref to the penalty box, and that was it. They helped Vleck off the ice, blood on his face, and I was given a five-minute major for fighting, Vleck got an instigator call. Amazing how I could make things look to the refs when I wanted to. The team captain shouted something at me in Russian, and Toly shrugged when I looked at him.

"Your mom," Toly explained.

I turned to face the massive Russian, who stared at

me with fire in his eyes, and then I shrugged. I'd done my bit, and the team could rally off it.

Ten was back on the ice. He skated by and nodded; I'd taken out their biggest, baddest D, and he was making me a promise that he would make it count.

Twenty-three seconds later, with a move that would make playoff highlight reels, a crisp pass from the captain, and Ten buried the puck past a startled, off-center goalie.

The fire of competition burned hot in the team, and suddenly we were winning. Two more, and we'd broken the opposition. Toly even snagged an empty-net goal when they took off their goalie.

We won the game, won this round and the newest expansion team had made it to the next stage of the Stanley Cup. It wasn't at home though, and the Washington crowd booed, but we'd had that all night; winning in the opposing team's arena is something we can all hope for in our careers. Ten skated in circles around me, and we head-bumped Stan, who couldn't stop grinning like an idiot.

Yeah. This was good.

And I needed to share that with someone. I needed to share all of this with Ben, who I knew had been watching.

We were staying at the hotel tonight, flying out in the morning, and the mood was high.

I didn't look at my phone. I didn't want anyone

else to see what he'd said, or what I was going to say back to him. I wanted complete privacy, just me and his words, and I would savor them and the fact we were on a win. I was stopped by team members, including Dieter who told me Lola sent her congratulations. I thanked him, standing patiently as he told me all about how he and Lola had placed bets on how many fights I would get into. He'd won, apparently, because Lola had assumed I would need to drop gloves at least three times to have any effect on the game.

Toly wanted to tell me how much of a dick Vleck was, and how pleased he was that I'd taken him out.

Ten wanted to high-five me, then do this complicated fist bump thing and explain to me how I needed to get a Pokémon tattoo.

Jared just shook my hand and nodded.

By the time I got back to my room I was a mess wanting to know what Ben had texted me. As soon as the door shut, I opened the phone and saw just two words.

Call me.

I stripped off my jacket, my belt, my tie and pants, and sat on my bed, pressing his number and not quite knowing what to say when Ben answered on the first ring.

"Fuck me," he said, uncharacteristically cursing, "That was intense," he added. "Congratulations."

I'd known I would love whatever he said, I just

hadn't known by how much. It wasn't the words; it was the breathlessness of the delivery, as if the game, or maybe me, had really blown him away.

"It was a good game—"

"Good? It was amazing. The way that you took Vleck out, oh my God, I've never seen him fall so fast, and then Ten, the way he took... Look, I'm officially a Railers fan for the rest of the Cup run."

I let him ramble on about Corsi scores, and twine, and lights, and the way Ten in his opinion would one day be captain, and how we missed Arvy but that it was okay because Dieter was a brilliant two-way forward. It went on and on, and I realized I was listening to a fanboy, and it made me smile. I was pulling Ben over from the dark side of supporting Washington, and if I had my way I would keep him.

Not for myself.

As a fan.

Of course.

He finally ran out of steam, and his voice dropped. "You know what I liked the most?"

I thought we'd covered everything, talking at length about my hit on Vleck, so it wasn't something to do with me, which left me a little disappointed until he started talking again.

"They showed the room post-game on Twitter. That bit when the Railers hand that blue hat to the MVP of the game? I know they gave it to Stan, but that should have gone to you, and then you went over to congratulate Stan…and…" He went quiet for a little while. "You'd taken your shirt off, and you stopped right in front of the camera, sweaty, your hair like you'd run your hands through it, and I've never seen anything so sexy."

Jeez. I was so hard, and I pushed my hand into my jersey shorts, wrapping my fingers around my aching cock. My man's voice was like fine whiskey, a burn and then a smooth warmth that flooded my system. I heard his breath hitch and I knew what he was doing.

"Are you getting yourself off?" I asked.

"When you turned to the camera and realized they'd caught you on camera, you flexed, I saw you, and the sweat, and…guh…"

I pushed at my shorts and tucked up my shirt, wishing I had more time—I wanted to prolong this—and I put him on speaker phone.

"What would you do?" I asked as I shuffled back on the bed, bending my legs and letting them fall to the sides. I set up a rhythm on my cock and closed my eyes.

"I'd just make you stand there," he said, his voice hitching again, "and I'd go to my knees, right there, and I'd suck you down so far…"

"Go on," I encouraged as he stopped.

"What would you do?" he said, throwing my question back at me.

God, how was I supposed to think? "I wouldn't let

you move. I'd hold your head still and I would fuck your mouth so hard…"

Silence, and then he groaned, and I knew that sound—it was him coming—and in seconds I was there with him, curling up into my fist then falling back on the bed, spent.

We were both quiet, and I don't know how long it lasted, but it was Ben who broke the silence.

"I've never done this before," he murmured, "but seeing you on the screen, and you winning…"

It sounded to me as if he was apologizing, what for I didn't know. Was it because it was a first for him? Or because he'd got turned on by a game?

"I've never had phone sex either, but hockey fights make me horny," I admitted, and I wasn't lying. I'd never made enough of a connection with a man to do something so incredibly intimate, but I was the first to admit I'd gotten off on a game before.

More silence, and I was just at the point of saying something stupid when he began to talk.

"It's not that I didn't have a healthy sex life with Liam; I did."

Do I want to hear this?

"It's just we were always with each other. We worked together, lived together, and I loved him so much, I didn't want to be away from him."

What does he want me to say to that?

"Uh-huh," I offered, because it was all I could think of. Part of me needed to hear him talk about his husband, because then he would see that what we had wasn't the same. It was just sex.

The other part of me ached for him, felt sorry for him, to have experienced such incredible, heart-breaking loss.

"I'm sorry he died," I added to my simple uh-huh; I think he needed to hear that.

"Thank you," he murmured. "I don't... I need..." He was clearly searching hard for the right words. "I'm sorry I ruined this," he finally said.

My stock response would be something crass about getting off to the sound of his voice, and to thank him for the fun. That was old Max. The Max that existed before I met Ben before he made me rethink what I was doing with myself.

Yes, I was retiring in a few weeks, yes, I was living with the fear of death hanging over me, but somehow Ben was reaching inside me, past all those knotted fears, and he was touching something icy and turning it hot.

So I rethought what I was going to say.

"You didn't ruin anything, Ben. I want you to talk to me. I need to know *you*."

Where those words came from, I didn't know. I just knew they were true.

WE HAD a few days off until our next game. Our opponents hadn't been decided; their games went to the full seven needed, and that meant when they met us in the next round they would be tired.

At least, that was what Coach Benton said, plainly, clearly, and without any hint of emotion. You'd think the man would be excited about getting this far in the playoffs, but he was calmly rational about the whole thing. Today he had us working on defending against Ten, which was an education in itself. The kid wasn't just fast, he had this way of looking at the ice, an awareness that had Westy and me dancing all over the place, not to mention Stan, who spent a lot of time patting his pipes in apology. The only time I actually stopped Ten was when I was catching a breather. He didn't realize I'd stopped and he ran into my motionless stance. He wasn't even breathing hard.

"My bad," he said, and broke off in the opposite direction.

"You think Jared puts speed in Ten's Wheaties?" Westy groused from next to me.

I tapped his shin with my stick. "Nah, we're just getting old."

"I'm twenty-four, asshole."

I leveled him a look. "Then yeah, you're just slow."

Westy huffed a laugh, and we took our positions, watching a grinning Ten stick-handling the puck in front of us. Damn kid was going to take us the whole way to the final, I knew it in my bones.

"Come take try goal," Stan shouted, his words

even more jumbled than usual. I admired the big guy, with his vocab out of a Russian spy film and his love of all things Erik.

"I'm two up," Ten yelled back.

Stan growled; I could hear it from there. "I let score. Make big ego." he said, determined, and took a stance.

And then Ten moved, from a standing start he flew; left, a wraparound, catching my stick with his, lifting it, driving the puck between Westy's legs, and he shot on the goal. Luckily, Stan was more observant and a lot faster than me and Westy, and he caught the puck, patting his pipes as he held it close to his chest like a kitten, hugging it protectively.

"You suck like Roomba suck rug!" he shouted at Ten.

I watched him and Ten chirping at each other, waited for the next D-pair to take their turn, then glanced up at the rafters. There were no retired jerseys there yet, and I doubted I would ever have my number retired after only being there a few months. Still, I would be part of this history-making team, and we were through to the next damn round.

Arvy skated over, still in the no-contact jersey. If he'd been healthy, then we would have had a formidable first line, unstoppable.

"How long now?" Westy asked, looking down at the injured leg as though he might be able to discern how the injury was. Then I realized I was doing the same thing.

Arvy shrugged. "Might get some ice time soon."

Ten snowed to a stop next to us. "You back for the next round?" He sounded hopeful, but Arvy didn't have anything to tell us.

Apart from one interesting thing.

"You're looking at Mister April," he said, and flexed his muscles. "I've still got it."

"July," Ten said. "They wanted me shirtless; Jared wasn't impressed."

I had no idea what they were talking about, but when Westy joined in to announce he was November and they wanted him to sit in fake snow, I was intrigued.

"It's the calendar for the shelter, the one where we're posing with the puppies as a fund-raiser. Ben is organizing it." Ten slid me a sly look as he said that.

Arvy piped up. "What month are you?"

"I have no idea." I doubted I would have been allocated anything. I was there for the Cup run, giving some depth and force, but after that I doubted the Railers would keep me on even if I wasn't going to retire anyway.

"He'll be October," Arvy said. "Give him some horns and he can be a devil."

"We should get them to paint him red," Westy added.

"I hate you all."

But at least the banter took the focus away from why I hadn't been given a month to pose for. I didn't want to talk about all that right now; my single-mindedness had to be on getting the Cup. As I showered, I thought about the rest of my day and felt peaceful.

Post-practice I was going to the shelter to catch up with Ben, we might even have an overnight stay where we actually managed to make love instead of falling asleep.

Life rocked.

And then, as I considered what I wanted out of tonight, I realized I hadn't thought about having sex with Ben. I'd thought about making love.

My head hurt.

Chapter Nine

Ben

"Benton, if you don't mind the hot dogs, they'll be char dogs."

I jumped a bit at Aunt Glenna's voice at my side. "Sorry, I was watching the kids playing street hockey."

I hurried to turn the wieners with my barbecue tongs as people milled around in my front yard, sipping lemonade and snacking on potato chips.

"Mmm-hmm. I'm sure it was the kids playing street hockey that had you all googly-eyed and dreamy."

My gaze flitted back to Max surrounded by a pack of inner-city kids playing hockey in the middle of the street. He was sweaty and tired, yet he laughed as loud as any of the poor children on that blacktop. Hardly any of them knew how to play hockey, but they were quick learners. Max had incredible patience and endless good humor. He was so different from the man who cruised the ice just looking for someone to knock ass-over-tin-cups. He filled my heart with things I'd thought I would never feel again. Things that made me giddy and hard and scared and kind of forgetful.

"Benton, the dogs?"

"Oh hell, right, sorry." I felt the blush creep up my neck. Aunt Glenna clucked her tongue, then fell into amused laughter. "Okay, fine, I might have been watching Max out there."

"He does look good in shorts and a tank top, but Lord the man needs some sun." She pattered off to check on the guests at this impromptu cookout. "Guests" meaning everyone in the neighborhood and "impromptu cookout" meaning block party to celebrate the Railers moving on to the conference championship against Florida. One more round, and they'd be playing for the Stanley Cup. I was so proud of Max, and his team. It was so exciting to be a part of the inner clique, even if I did make for one funny sort of WAG.

Aunt Carol appeared on my left, chewing on a carrot stick. "Don't leave them on too long, Benton. No one likes them burned."

I looked down at the old woman beside me. "Who exactly is wearing the apron that reads B-B-Q KING on it?" I tapped the apron tied around my waist with my tongs. "Yeah, that's right. Me. So go worry over something else."

"You're a sassy-ass today." She snorted and poked me with her carrot before wandering off to socialize.

I loved those two old women. They'd set this whole thing up and never once let it slip to me. That was impressive stuff, because there was nothing my aunts liked better than gossiping. Well, aside from sticking it to the man, that is.

"How are the hot dogs coming along?" I was ready to snap at whomever was asking about the dogs. I was the barbecue king. I knew how to roast a wiener. "Or is that a bad thing to ask?"

"No, sir, it's a fine thing to ask." I smiled at my pastor and hoped thinking bad thoughts about him wouldn't get me on the wrong side of the Lord. Pastor Bert—and yes, Bert is his last name; his first name is Alabaster—was a tall man, lean, gray-haired, and always smiling. He'd lost his wife of forty-nine years two years ago, and so now everyone who attended the Rose of Beulah Baptist Church was trying to find him a girlfriend. Kind of how they'd tried to find me a boyfriend after Liam had died.

"I take it everyone is worried about the hot dogs?" he asked, mischief in his eyes.

"You could say that." I chuckled and rolled the dogs over.

"People do like to nose around," he commented as his gaze went to the kids and Max playing on the blocked-off street. "I was glad to see your new friend at services. He seems a fine man."

"Yes, sir, he is that."

"You do realize he's welcome in our house of worship any time?"

"Yes, sir, I do. And thank you for always being open to me and others in the LGBTQ community."

Pastor Bert smiled at me, and you could see the love for his work right there in his eyes.

"Benton, the Lord loves all his children. As his servant, it would be an affront not to love them all as well." He patted my shoulder then leaned in. "Besides, I'm hoping to maybe get a few tickets for the youth group for a game next season."

That made me laugh out loud. "I'll have Max tell someone to call you."

"Thank you. Don't be late for choir practice next week. I'm off to check out the baked goods. Clara Miller said she was bringing her famous chocolate cake. I am a weak man in the face of chocolate cake."

I hoped he kept that weakness to himself. Clara was a widow and a prime candidate for new girlfriend material.

Max and the kids all whooped. Someone must have scored. His gaze found me across the yard and among all the neighbors. There was fire in those stunning eyes of his. I stared at him for the longest time, until someone shouted that the hot dogs were on fire.

Then I attended to the cooking and not my man. I'd have to attend to him later.

AS SOON AS the door to my house was shut, I was attending to my man. And Max, it seemed, was all about being attended to.

I pressed his back to the wall, the fridge kicking on beside us. "Sitting there all night and looking at you and not being able to crawl all over you was torture." I shoved that sexy damn tank top up to his chin, my fingers slipping through the curls on his chest while my lips settled over his mouth. Max was hard and ready, his hands coming up to cradle my head as I ground my dick against his. I plucked at his nipples as he sucked on my tongue.

"Thank goodness DK asked to spend the night with Carol and Glenna," he panted between hot, wet kisses.

"I paid him five bucks to stay the night." I shoved my hand into his shorts.

"I gave him twenty."

We both softly laughed, then broke apart long enough to rush to the bedroom. Bucky had gone to bed in his crate all by himself. He lay there, head on his paws, tail gently thumping his thick cushion.

"You're a good boy," I whispered. I gave him a treat, then closed and locked the crate. Max was waiting for me by the stairs, wearing a tender smile.

He offered me his hand. I took it and led him to my bed.

Once we stepped into my room, things sort of changed. The air around us shifted, or maybe it was a subtle change in our auras. Hell, I don't know what it was, but there was a softness about the way we touched and tasted each other that I'd not felt before. His hands reverently moved over my skin, his mouth brushed my neck.

"What do you want from me tonight, Ben?" Max slipped between my legs, caging me, hands on either side of my head, his cock like a branding iron resting beside mine. "Tell me what you want from me."

There were a million things I could have said... perhaps *should* have said. I could have told him I wanted him to love me and not just fuck me. I should have told him that I wanted him to care about me as much as I had grown to care about him.

"Wake up with me." That was all I dared to say.

He kissed me breathless, then folded my legs up and across my chest, hooking my ankles, allowing his cock to slip down over my balls.

"I'd love to wake up with you," he replied, the words thick with desire. I let my eyes drift shut as he tore open a condom packet then pumped some lube into his hand. Hearing him coat his cock sent a ripple of white-hot lust through me. "You ready for me?"

"Lord, yes," I panted as I clawed at his sides.

He slid into me in one long, smooth thrust. When

he was as deep as he could go, he pressed my legs more firmly to my chest and began moving. He flicked his hips quickly—short, deep drives that stole my breath while pushing me far too rapidly to a climax. Damn the man, he knew just how to move, how to pump those hips of his, how to fondle my balls and stroke my cock.

"Is this what you need from me, Ben?"

"Yes…yes…yes."

My orgasm hit me hard. I arched up, fell back, and shouted his name. His right hand held my kicking cock, his left kept my legs pinned to my chest. I came all over my lower abdomen and calves. Max ground into me. I yelped at the depth and the pressure. Then he tumbled over his own summit, his growls of completion making me shudder. He dropped my cock and fell beside me on the bed, his cock sliding out of me. Straightening my legs was painful yet glorious.

Max said nothing for the longest time. I slid from the bed to find a dirty shirt to clean off with as he took care of the condom. He reached for me when I returned to the bed, pulling me to him. We lay looking at each other. I thought I could see it in his eyes. That emotion that we all searched for. That glowing feeling that lyricists wrote songs about and poets waxed eloquently over. I knew I was feeling it. I thought I was feeling it. Maybe I was just seeing the love growing inside me for this man reflected in his eyes. Perhaps I was projecting, or it might be wishful thinking.

"You okay?" he asked a moment later. I nodded and smiled and brushed away all that sentimental stuff. "You look funny."

"That's my lingering orgasm face," I quipped. "You look funny too."

"Can't help that, I was born with this face."

That made me snicker. "I like your face." I wiggled closer, and he draped a thick arm over my shoulder.

"I like your face too."

WORK WAS one thing that kept my mind off missing Max and the constant concern over Rolf. The man had been too quiet. I suspected he was biding his time to drag out the torture. I'd even called one of the cops I knew and discussed the situation with him. Unless DK was willing to press charges, they really couldn't do anything. His advice had been to be careful and call if he showed up.

That sat there on the back-burner in my mind like a rancid kettle of lamb stew. Sadly, I didn't even have Max there to help ease the disquiet.

He and the Railers were resting, ready for the first two games of the conference championship against Florida. Thankfully they were starting at home, but we didn't meet up. We talked as often as work, practice, and the press corps would allow. The media pressure was insane. So far, I'd managed to stay out of the limelight, and that was okay. I'd only seen my name linked with him once on a small sports blog DK had pointed out to me.

I had no issue with being seen at his side. I'd come out long ago. I'd been married and openly run Crossroads with Liam. So, the thought of cameras in my face was nothing that worried me. It was just the intensity of the media and the fans as the teams battled to the final round. Some of the stuff I read online aimed at the players horrified me. And the vile hatred thrown at Tennant Rowe because he loved a man saddened me deeply. I would never understand how those who claimed they were children of Christ could warp the words of a man who preached love into such twisted hate.

The shelter had been inundated with new intakes. We now had so many kittens it was hard to find room for them all. Four dogs had been rescued, one in such bad shape there was no saving the starving little thing and our vet had kindly put him down. We had a little poodle mix who had been so dirty and matted we'd had to shave her down to the skin. She'd be a hard sell to people without her pretty brown curls, so that meant she'd be here for quite some time. I spent another hour after closing trying to make the money stretch far enough, but it just wasn't happening.

"Dammit all." I sighed, pushing back from my

desk. My eyes were scratchy, my back stiff, and my heart heavy. We'd need to put on another major fundraiser to cover costs next month. Since we had so little cash in the coffers, I'd have to dip into my savings for some of the necessities, like advertising. Bucky wiggled up next to me, his blue eyes questioning. "I wish I'd been born rich instead of so damn good-looking."

His tail wagged merrily at my joke.

"Let's go check on Cocoa, then go home."

Bucky raced to the office door then ran to the kennels. I left him outside despite his sad looks. New intakes were kept away from other dogs for a reason.

Cocoa—who was not very cocoa-colored without her fur—scrabbled across the tiles, tiny butt wiggling and bare tail whipping. She seemed comfortable enough. Thank God it was late spring and not winter. Poor tiny thing would be freezing.

She bounded after the treat I tossed into her kennel, ate it, and curled back up on her cushion. Bucky glared at me when I exited the runs.

"Sorry, you'll be able to visit her soon." I snapped his leash on and led him outside, locking the door and engaging the security system.

Bucky sat beside me, tongue lolling, snout out the window, enjoying the wind in his face. If only life were as easy for us humans. I really missed having someone waiting for me at home. I missed sitting down to a meal with a man who asked me how things were going. Those little things were massive when they were gone from your life. A gentle reminder to pay the water bill, to pick up some milk.

"Do we need milk?"

Bucky sneezed, filling the incoming air with dog snot.

"I'll take that as a no."

Pulling up in front of our row of brick houses, I saw the lights were off at my aunts'. There was a school board meeting tonight. They'd probably dragged DK with them to that. They liked having him chauffeur them around. Truthfully, DK driving eased my mind a bit. Both of my aunts had dinged several cars in the past year. And I kind of hoped he was with them, because I loved the kid, but my mood was sour tonight, my back bowed with worry about work and the want of something more in my personal life. A warm meal, a cold beer, and a long shower might help lift the blues. I spied my running shoes in the closet when I hung up Bucky's leash. A run. Yeah, that might help. Bucky and I could go over to Wildwood Lake, work up a good sweat, and maybe take a break on the same bench Max and I had had a sort-of date on.

I liked that idea a lot. After a quick change into running shorts and a Railers tank top—my friends back in D.C. would never forgive me—and a note slid under my aunts' door telling them where I was and when I hoped to be back, I loaded Bucky back up and we were off.

As soon as I felt the crunch of gravel under my sneakers and the twinge of thigh muscles responding, I knew this had been a good idea. Sure, it was hot, and I was already sweating, but sweat was good. Sweat was worry leeching out of your pores. Bucky jogged along at my side, happy to be active. Dogs like him weren't made to lie around in offices all day. I was a bad doggy daddy as well as a crummy boyfriend. If I was a boyfriend at all, which I didn't think I was. Max seemed to be in no hurry to commit. Should I drop a hint? Maybe I should ask him out on a date. A real date. Not a sex date. Something romantic. Sweat ran into my eyes as we ran past the wetland area, the song of tiny frogs warming up for the nighttime concerto filling the humid air.

My legs burned and my lower back was tight, but I was starting to feel better. I would ask Max out. On a dinner date. In a restaurant. With other people. And I would hold his hand and tell him I not only liked his face, I kind of loved it. Then we could go home and have sex. Yeah. Smiling despite the tug of my hamstrings complaining, I rounded a corner, and there stood Rolf, leaning against a thick oak tree.

Had he followed me to the park? What possible reason could he have for being at a random park the same time as I was?

I skidded to a halt, Bucky tight to my side. Seeing

Rolf there, with the shadows of the setting sun falling over him, I thought I was seeing a ghost. Liam and he looked so alike they'd been mistaken for twins a few times. Anger and fear welled up inside me. I tightened my grip on Bucky's leash. The dog began to whimper, unsure and upset about the dark feelings flowing out of me.

"Are you following me?" I panted. He rolled a lip. How could anyone mistake him for his kind, loving, caring younger brother was beyond me. You could see the hatred in his light blue eyes. "DK is not going back home."

"As if I wanted the bastard back under my roof. You've probably already turned him, just like you did Liam." He never moved, just stood there, nonchalantly leaning on that damn tree, appearing to be just a guy talking to another guy should anyone run past.

"What do you want?"

"I want what's mine. What Liam was going to leave me until you wormed your faggot ass into his head and twisted him up."

I sorely wished I could keep my emotions under control as Rolf was doing. Aside from the burn of revulsion in his gaze, he was as cool as that proverbial cucumber. Handsome, yes, and unassuming in manner.

"What kind of shit are you talking here?"

Bucky growled low in his chest. I did not tell him to stop.

"I want half of Liam's assets. Just like I would have gotten if not for you turning him."

My mouth dropped open a bit. What assets? The only thing he'd had was his half of the investment in the shelter, and that had become mine when he passed away.

"You're out of your mind."

A young woman ran past. Rolf smiled warmly at her. She nodded back.

"Pretty, huh? Oh yeah, that's right. Your kind don't like tits and pussy."

"I'm done with you. If you want money, get a loan. You're not getting shit from me. Liam and I were married. Legally. Everything that was his became mine. And what was mine would have gone to him if I'd died."

"You dying. Yeah, that can be arranged." He threw my snarling dog a murderous look, then ambled off, the lowering sun making his shadow long and distorted.

The sweat beaded up on my neck slithered down my spine, chilling me. Had he just threatened me? I stood there for a long time, staring at where Rolf had been, shivering despite it being close to eighty degrees out. That bastard had just threatened me.

"Sweet Jesus," I mumbled, fear gripping me tightly around the throat. I dug into the pocket of my running shorts and called the person I needed to talk to the most. Max.

Chapter Ten

Max

We'd agreed not to meet up tonight. The day after tomorrow was our first game against Florida, and Tampa Bay were coming off a full seven-game battle to get to this round against us. I'd made the very adult decision of resting up tonight, and promptly missed the hell out of Ben. I'd watched some shit film on Netflix, too wired to watch something good, too distracted to stand up and get the remote control, which had fallen off the side of the sofa and out of my reach. Ben had actually bet me that I couldn't go one night without sex; the amount on the table was ten dollars. I wasn't going to lose.

Practice today had been odd-man rushes; we were shit-hot on those, and Stan still hadn't let anything in. As a team we were positive, and there was a cautious excitement in the room. I could focus on hockey, think about hockey, anything not to think about Ben and sex.

Still, I wished Ben were there, or that I was at Ben's because he had this way of calming me down and centering me. Of giving me a purpose outside hockey that wasn't just sex.

I was hoping he'd call at some point, like a love-sick teenager, but he hadn't so far. Apart from one random text about waiting in line at Walmart, there had been radio silence. He really was taking me at my word that I needed to sleep and focus on the next game where we had home-ice advantage. Yesterday's barbecue had been an eye-opener. Most of the team had attended, although no one had eaten anything that could remotely give them food poisoning, just in case.

When the phone rang, I dived for it, connecting the call before it reached my ear.

"I knew you'd phone," I crowed triumphantly. "That's ten you owe me."

"Max."

The tone shut me down, cut my good humor to nothing, and I sat up from my slouch.

"Ben? What's wrong?"

"I shouldn't have called," he said after a small silence.

Fuck this. I was up and pulling on a jacket, passing my phone from one hand to the other, always keeping it at my ear.

"What's wrong?" I asked again, and pushed my feet into my sneakers, shuffling around until they fit properly. My chest was tight. "Is it the shelter? Has someone broken in again?"

I'd spoken to the security company, and they'd assured me they'd upped their systems and added in some drive-by's. I couldn't help feeling as if it wasn't just the shelter that was being targeted, and I didn't like it one little bit.

"No."

His voice was small, and I grabbed my keys even as I listened to what he wasn't saying. There was fear in his tone, and I wasn't ready to sit there and just listen to that. I was out of the door within a minute and standing outside Westy's apartment. He had a unit in the same building as me, rented, both of us unsure of our permanent place on the team. Of course, Westy would be picked up—he was fucking awesome. But I was done. I needed to be done.

I knocked on his door even as I spoke to Ben.

"Where are you?"

"I came home," he said.

"I'll be there in ten."

A sleepy-looking Westy answered the door, and it looked like he was going to curse me out at first for waking him up, and then his expression changed when he got a good look at me.

"What's wrong?" he asked, looking past me, probably expecting some disaster where he could see it.

"I need you to drive me somewhere."

He didn't argue. I was acting like a madman, but he still grabbed his keys and we took the stairs to the parking lot.

I didn't want to drop the call. "Talk to me, Ben," I pleaded.

Westy side-eyed me as we pulled out of the parking lot, but I wasn't about to explain.

"I'll wait for you," Ben said, sounding regretful, then he disconnected the call.

"Ben? Ben!"

This wasn't right. This was so far from right.

"Where am I going?" Westy asked at the exit to our building. I needed to get my head around which direction we needed.

"Ben's place. You remember where it is?" Westy had been at the barbecue, but would he recall the intricate directions to get there again? He reached over and selected the last destination in his navigation system, and I didn't have to give him any directions at all.

Westy never questioned me once. Luckily, the roads to Ben's place were deserted for the longest time until we entered the neighborhood and slowed to almost nothing before parking outside his place. There was no sign of his aunts' cars, and I hoped to hell it wasn't one of them who'd been hurt or died or something. Westy followed me out of the car. I didn't stop him; hell, I wasn't sure what I was going to find.

Ben opened the door as we reached it, and fuck, he looked shaken.

We stepped in, Westy shut the door behind us, and I managed to get Ben in my arms all in the same weirdly coordinated action.

"What happened?" I asked again, and Ben gripped my shirt tighter and buried his face in my neck. Westy slid past us and disappeared into a small kitchen, coming back with a bottle of whiskey and a glass. He gestured to the living room, and I carefully, slowly, guided Ben into the room and sat him on the sofa. He pulled me down with him, and Westy took a seat on the coffee table in front of us.

I wasn't convinced I wanted Westy seeing Ben like this. Shouldn't I be protecting Ben from someone seeing him so damn vulnerable?

"What happened?" Westy asked, his tone firmer than I could have used given that my worry was all wrapped up in fear.

"I think…" Ben looked up at me and grasped my hands. "Rolf."

Okay, this wasn't the shelter, this was that asshole Rolf, DK's father, the one who'd beaten his own son. Hell, wait, was this about DK? I looked around me as if I was expecting DK to appear from nowhere, just to reassure me he was okay.

Nothing.

"Is it DK? Is he hurt?"

Ben shook his head. "He's out with my aunts, and then staying at Skipper's house," he murmured. "Rolf doesn't know where that is."

"What did Rolf do, then?"

"I think... I'm being stupid... He couldn't have..."

Ben stopped and stared at Westy, almost like it was the first time he realized it wasn't just him and me in the room, and he tensed. Westy met his gaze.

"Is this a police matter?" Westy asked.

Ben nodded, and Westy was dialing 9-1-1 before I could get to my own phone.

"Police," Westy said into the receiver. He looked up, abruptly realizing he didn't know what the hell he was asking for.

"Rolf threatened me," Ben murmured.

Something roared inside me, and at that moment I wanted to hunt Rolf down and kill him; tear him limb from limb and leave the parts of him in with the dogs. I'd never felt such a murderous rage before, and it left me feeling dizzy with the force of it. I couldn't hear what Westy was explaining, such was the sound in my head. I pushed Ben away from me a little and turned to face him.

"Tell me everything," I snapped.

His eyes widened, and if I'd been in less of a temper, or if fear hadn't stolen my rational side, then maybe I would have seen I was losing control.

He edged away from me, but I gripped his arm. "I'll kill him."

He attempted to shake free, but all I knew was that I couldn't take my hands from him, that I needed that connection.

"Max," he said, and shook his arm again. "You're scaring me."

I instantly let go and scooted away from him a little. Shit, I was no better than the asshole who'd threatened him.

"I'm sorry," I said, and held up my hands. Westy passed the whiskey to Ben, and I stared at him as he sipped it and then downed the whole lot in one go. Jesus. "Will you tell me...?"

"He says he wants..." Ben glanced at Westy, who nodded in understanding.

"I'm making coffee," he announced, and vanished into the kitchen.

Ben gestured at the retreating figure. "Were you with him?"

"With Westy? No, I knocked on his door and got him to drive me over."

"Oh."

Silence again.

"Tell me what Rolf did."

Ben massaged his temples and shut his eyes. "I don't even recall half of it, but he said—at least I think he said—that killing me was an option to get what he wanted."

The dragon inside me roared loudly again, and I had to physically make myself stay where I was. The cops were the right people to tell. They would come here, make sense of all this, arrest Rolf, and put everything to rights.

"What do you mean, you think you know what he said?" I asked after a little while.

"It wasn't so much what he said, but the way he said it, and he smiled at this woman who jogged past and anyone looking would think it was just two guys talking, but Bucky didn't like it."

None of that made sense, except maybe for the Bucky part. I spotted him in the crate in the corner, curled in a ball, his gaze fixed firmly on me and Ben.

"He knew I was upset, so I thought I'd put him in his bed," Ben explained, then edged closer to me. I pulled him in for a sideways hug and we waited for the cops in silence.

They arrived at the same time as coffee, and then I had to listen to the story of how that asshole Rolf had likely followed Ben to the park, intimidated him, implied that the way he'd get what he thought he was owed was over Ben's dead body. I attempted to stay quiet, held him as he talked, and then when it all got too much and I wanted to hit something, I eased myself away.

Standing with Westy, watching Ben explain, I *really* wanted to hit something. Someone. Anyone.

The cops were thorough. They documented it all,

took notice of what Ben was saying. They couldn't do much about what Ben *thought* Rolf had meant, but they updated their records. When they left, it was me who shook their hands, and me who tidied up the coffee mugs. Westy left soon after, not even asking if I wanted to be driven home. He knew the score as much as I did.

I took Ben to bed, undressed him carefully, gently laid him down, and held him close.

I didn't sleep until I heard his even breaths, and I spent most of that time staring at the picture of Ben and his husband, Liam, which was no longer face down.

If Liam was looking down at him now and seeing what an asshole his brother was, I bet he wanted to come back as an avenging angel or some shit like that. I could have reached over and turned the frame, but it didn't freak me out to see Ben so happy with his husband. If anything, it was comforting to think that I could look out for Ben here, and maybe Liam could keep an eye on him from *up there*.

When I woke, he was gone, but I heard the noise in the kitchen, smelled the coffee, and he seemed calmer than last night.

"Maybe I overreacted," he suggested.

"Things always look better in daylight," I said. "Doesn't mean they weren't awful in the dark."

I wasn't sure if that was the right thing to say, but

he hugged me, we kissed, and he promised to be careful at the shelter that day.

PRACTICE WAS A BASTARD. It didn't help I was low on sleep and trying to defend against Ten, but I was as useless as a five-year-old on the ice. So much so that Jared called me on it and took me off the ice.

"What the hell?" he asked as we headed for the locker room.

"Didn't sleep so good."

Something in my tone must have told him a story of sorts. He didn't get in my face about protecting Ten, or keeping my fists up, or not slashing the opposition and drawing stupid penalties. He ordered me to the showers and told me to go home.

I promised I would.

I lied.

The shelter was quiet, and I found Ben with the puppies, my man on the floor hugging each puppy that wanted it. He looked up when I walked in and he grinned at me.

Seemed there was nothing in this world that was so bad a puppy couldn't fix it.

I joined him on the floor and we chatted about hockey, the Cup, the shelter, puppies, and that time I lost two teeth to a hundred-mile-an-hour puck to the jaw.

Not once did we talk about Rolf or his threats, but

I made damn sure to mention everything to the security company, and I also might have hired someone to watch the place and keep an eye on Ben. Just in case.

He didn't need to know that, though.

SECOND PERIOD of our first game against Florida, and I really wished they'd benched me. I'd already spent time in the penalty box, twice, for infractions that had been accidents, not deliberate in any way. My head was messed up and I needed to get back in the game, because I was not going to be the one responsible for the Railers not getting to the final. Seven games in this round, and all we had to do was win four of them. The Stanley Cup was tantalizingly close.

I felt the tap on my shoulder, didn't even have to look up to know it was Jared. Mads was living up to his name; I could see the tension bracketing his mouth and the confusion in his eyes.

I nodded at him. I knew what he was going to say. This was a tied game at two goals each, and we were so evenly matched it was painful to see. We had more chances, but their goalie was on form and nothing was going in.

All he did was nod back, and when I went over the boards for the next shift, I was focused on the hockey and not on Ben.

The game was ragged. Neither team seemed to

have the edge, and there was a randomness to the shots that went into the net. Lucky bounces, hits on the goalies, the net coming off the moorings that held it in place on two separate occasions. The mood was of confusion and madness, and it wasn't too long before the consistent targeting of our forwards paid off for the other team.

When I saw their D-man push Ten into the boards, I was relieved. Not that Ten was hurt—which he wasn't, because he clambered to stand very quickly —but because I had a legitimate reason to pummel on someone.

Getting sent to the bin for a two-minute roughing call, I at least felt I had worked out some of the tension inside me. In fact, I was grinning and chirping at Tampa's D-man, who shouted obscenities at me.

Until the crowd roared, and I looked back at the game. Ten on a breakaway, Ten dazzling the crowd. I could feel the goal on its way, and I stood up, watching. But I could see the Tampa captain, heading right for Ten, just as fast, but the trajectory was wrong. I shouted at Westy to get between them, but he wasn't placed right where I would have been. Ten was open, vulnerable, and then time slowed for me. With the chilling certainty that they would collide, I couldn't help the curse of complete horror that left my mouth. Ten must have caught on at the last moment—at least his head was up—but the impact of the two men colliding, sliding into the wall, was enough to silence the arena. A tangle of arms and legs, the two men were utterly still for a moment, and then everything sped up again, the teams rushing to the two of them, helping them to stand.

Fuck. Was Ten injured because I'd felt it so fucking necessary to beat on someone? Was I that much of a Neanderthal the only way I could handle my own pain was to dish out pain to others? I held my breath. I think the entire arena held their breath.

And then Ten was standing, shoving at Tampa's captain and chirping at him. I didn't see that happen much with Ten—he was too fast to get caught normally—but to see him standing toe to toe with the guy who'd taken him off his skates had me grinning like an idiot. I looked at the bench, watching Mads standing there with his arms crossed over his chest. I willed him to stare at me, to connect with me over the fact Ten was okay. He didn't look my way once, but he did squeeze my shoulder when I was back on the bench. He knew what it was like to be in the bin watching the guys you were protecting left vulnerable.

Which just circled my brain back to Ben.

We won the game, but it was only a rebound goal off their goalie's blocker that took us to victory. There was nothing clever about that night's game, no finesse.

As soon as I could, I checked my cell. Ben couldn't come to tonight's game—he had a shift to cover at the shelter—but DK was with him, and the security company assured me everything was quiet.

There was a text from Ben, a congratulation with an added kiss. And weirdly, one from my mom, who suggested we should soundly beat Tampa quickly, almost as if she knew what she was talking about. I sent her back a promise we would, then turned my attention to Ben's text. I considered what to write but could think of absolutely nothing.

So, I did what any self-respecting lover did when he wanted to talk to his partner.

I grabbed a cab and made my way to the shelter. No game tomorrow, no practice, just optional skate.

And tonight, I really wanted to spend time with Ben.

Chapter Eleven

Ben

I waited for Max to arrive. I knew he'd show up. Call it a hunch or the Force or a good guess, but I could feel him coming closer. Imagine his shock when he showed up at the locked gates of the shelter and I was waiting for him, motor running, ready to take him on a real date.

"Hey," he cautiously said while paying and tipping the driver.

"Hey yourself," I replied, ass resting on the bumper of my car, arms crossed, the ultimate picture of Mr. Cool. If only my interior was as chill as my exterior. My stomach was a jumble of nerves, my heart was skipping a beat, by the feels, and my cock was plumping up just looking at the man in his suit and tie.

Max looked through the gates at the shelter. Crickets chirruped and a dog barked. The air was heavy with humidity. The steady hum of city traffic surrounded us.

"What's going on?" He pulled his blue tie out from under his shirt collar and shoved it into his front pocket. Then the jacket was removed, showing off thick arms wrapped in soft cotton.

"We're going on a date."

He glanced back at me, one eyebrow climbing upward.

"We are?"

"Yes. We are." I opened the passenger side door for him. "We have to hurry, though. It closes at ten."

"Uh, that only gives us about forty minutes." Max showed me the heavy watch on his left wrist.

"Which is why I'm telling you to hurry." I waved a hand at my car's interior.

"Wait," Max looked around him. "I thought DK was with you."

"He was. Now he's not." Another jerky motion at the open door.

He walked over and got into the car. I shut the door like a real gentleman, then raced around the front of the Jeep and dove behind the wheel.

"Good thing the game didn't go into overtime," I said, pulling away with my confused date at my right. I turned up the stereo and Teddy Pendergrass oozed out of the speakers.

"Good thing." Max buckled up, then hit me with a firm look. "What is all this about?"

"It's about the fact we've never had a date." I glanced quickly at him, then back at the road. Teddy was crooning about turning out the lights. Mm-mm-mm, that sounded good. Me, Max, a bed, and a dark room. Or a room with lights. I was good with either scenario.

No, dammit. No. This is a no-sex date night. Be strong, Benton!

"I didn't know we were doing the whole dating thing."

Worry set in. I concentrated on the traffic leaving the city.

"I didn't either at first." I'd decided to be honest with the man. He had always been one hundred percent honest with me. No false promises or honeyed words to get me into bed. Not that he'd needed them, but still…

"And now you think you want the dating thing."

"If you do." *Argh. No, that was backpedaling. Be strong, Benton!* "I mean yeah. I want to date you."

I jerked my chin up a bit as I zipped along, my speed maybe a bit higher than it legally should be.

"Huh."

I threw him a look, but he seemed well and truly into himself, so I let that admission bounce around the inside of the Jeep as we hightailed it to Hershey.

When we pulled up at the park, Max's bushy

eyebrows knotted up. "So we busted ass to get to an amusement park?"

"Well…yeah." I threw open the door and got out of the car. He did the same. I checked my watch. I'd made the twenty-five-minute drive in less than twenty, so we had about fifteen minutes before the park closed for the night. "There's something impor-tant I wanted to say to you in a special place. Come on."

Max muttered something under his breath. What it was, I didn't know, but we ran to the gates, paid to get in, and hustled past roller coasters and water rides, breathlessly arriving at the Kissing Tower with just ten minutes to closing.

"I'm going to pass out," Max panted as the disgruntled park employee ushered us into the rotating cabin. We were the only ones on the ride, which was good. I'd been hoping for a little privacy for my great confession. Also, if Max blew me off, no one would be there to see me cry.

"Don't pass out yet." I took his hand and led him to one of the candy-kiss-shaped windows. The ride started quickly, probably because the employees wanted to go home. Up the cabin rose, two hundred and fifty feet into the air, as it slowly rotated. We sat down and looked out the candy-shaped windows, working to catch our breath.

"This is really something," Max said as the cabin slowly turned, showing those inside a panoramic view of the illuminated park and the lights of downtown Hershey. My gaze was on him.

"Yeah, it really is."

He turned on the padded bench and settled his beautiful brown-gold eyes on me.

I leaned in and kissed him. We *were* in the kissing tower, after all. He responded with simmering heat that was evident and burbling below the surface.

I cupped his face, the rough scratch of his beard on my palms crazy pleasant.

"I really like you and I want to date you. In public. Holding hands and whispering over a candlelight meal sort of dating."

He seemed to digest that news slowly. The cabin continued to rotate. My belly felt a little queasy, and not from the mellow ride we were on.

"Okay, I'd like that too."

He hauled me to him, plastering his mouth over mine. Somehow, by the time the cabin was back on the ground, I'd been pulled onto his lap, facing him, and was having my neck feasted on by a ravenous hockey player.

The doors opening on the cabin and the shout from a disgruntled park worker broke into the sensual moment. I leaped up, we both shoved at our erections, and we exited the ride looking rather sheepish. Max took my hand. That made me feel lighter than I had since Rolf had threatened me.

"Okay, you lost that loving look. What's wrong?"

"Just thinking about Rolf."

"Did you hear from him again?"

"No, no, he's not that stupid." We were shown out of the park and walked to my Jeep, fingers woven together, giving me strength that I gladly soaked up. "Let's not talk about that hateful bastard. Tonight is supposed to be about us. DK and my aunts are down in D.C., so I don't have to fret over them."

"What are they doing down there?"

He led me to the car, then eased my back to the driver's side door, stepping up nice and close, pressing his chest to mine.

"They wanted to take him to his first sit-in. Protesting for women's rights." He nudged at my jaw with his nose, intent on getting back to tasting my neck. I let him nibble. It was just him and me and a thousand moths flitting about under the light over-head. "Mmm, that's so nice. Want to find a place to eat then go back to my place?"

His head came up quickly. "I think Stan lives around here." He gave the parking lot a look. "I mean, not here, obviously, but in Hershey. Maybe we could stop by and have a drink. Might be nice to spend some time with another couple."

"Yeah, that would be nice. Where does he live?"

"Somewhere in Hershey. Big gates, according to Lockhart. We can just cruise around until we find it." He buried his face back in my neck. I shook my head.

He sighed and pulled back to look at me. "No, you don't want to visit Stan?"

"Oh, I do, I just need you to think about what you just suggested. You said that *I* should cruise around an affluent neighborhood, after dark, checking out the rich folks' houses."

He mulled it over for about five seconds, then his brows untangled.

"Oh," he murmured.

"Yeah."

"That truly sucks."

"Tell me. So, how about we skip that possibly unpleasant scenario and just go find a quiet place to eat then go home."

"Italian. I'm hungry for Italian. And you."

I was hungry for him too, but fettuccine did sound good. "We could get it to go."

"What about the real date?"

"We rode a ride. That technically constitutes a real date."

You're a weak, weak man, Benton.

His chuckle was rich. "That we did. Takeout it is."

WE TOOK our takeout to my bed. We lay among tin foil pans filled with fettuccine Alfredo, lasagna, and spaghetti and meatballs, nude, feeding each other between long, sloppy kisses. Pasta began to slide from our forks, long strands slithering down my side to the sheets, or fat, round meatballs rolling down Max's hip to rest beside his hard cock. I sucked on a pair of meaty balls—all covered with red sauce rich with garlic. Max snorted and chuckled throughout, his hair and beard thick with sauce, my chest and dick coated with rich, cheesy Alfredo sauce.

The covers were a mess, the sheets stained and ruined, but we rolled around in the seasoned sauces anyway, play giving way to passion as one hunger bowed to another.

Lubing up his ass was sloppy fun. I pushed my fingers deeply into him as I sucked on the fat head of his prick. Max tugged and pulled until I was straddling him, my knees on either side of his head. He greedily took me into his mouth. Two fat fingers coated with lube and probably Alfredo sauce found my ass. I rocked back onto those eager fingers, gasping around his cock as he hooked them perfectly and stroked my sweet spot. I got lost in Max, and it was just what I needed. Loving the man wiped the worry from my mind. There was no Rolf, no elderly aunts, no teenaged boy alone and unwanted by his family, and no shelter teetering on the edge of foreclosure. For this one wonderful short span of time, it was just me and Max.

He came first, coating my tongue and throat. I shuddered wickedly, the heady taste of him combined with the scratch of his fingers along my prostate pushing me over the edge. Max hummed and suckled, never pulling off or gagging, taking my wild thrusts while working my ass madly.

"Hell...oh hell." He held me tightly, one hand on my ass, keeping me from moving away until he was done. Each pull of his lips over my cock got him another shudder. Finally he let me break free and fall by him on the bed. An aluminum pan flipped up and coated my back with some cold, wet noodle nasty.

"Ah, man," I coughed, curling into a small ball as the last little tremors rolled through me.

"My spaghetti," Max moaned. He rolled me onto my stomach and ate his dinner from my lower back as I snickered and giggled.

"You're the tastiest plate ever invented," he purred as he covered me with his bulk, his chest pressing me into the saucy bedding.

I lifted a hand in defeat and was flipped onto my back, pan collapsing as my ass flattened it.

His laughing gaze found mine.

"You're very special to me," I whispered, then flicked a tiny chunk of meatball from his beard.

"You're very special to me too," he replied, dipping his head to take a long taste of my mouth that ended up leading us into my bathroom, which led us into another round of lovemaking in the skinny shower.

After that, we were ready for bed. One that wasn't coated with the dinner specials from Lou's Ristorante over on Locust Street. We crashed in the guest bedroom, kicking the soda cans from DK's bed to the floor and falling asleep as soon as we were cuddled close with our heads on the pillows.

Overall, for a first real date, I was damn happy with the outcome, even if I did slip up a bit on the no sex thing.

THE OLD GALS and DK had opted to stay in D.C. for a few days. Thankfully, the protest had been a peaceful one. I'd joked with my father that if they ended up in the slammer it was on him to bail them out. He'd laughed, but it hadn't been a heartfelt laugh. He knew how those two were.

So that left me alone at the next Railers game. I was late arriving due to some new intakes and a sick cat issue combined with some sort of call from the Department of Agriculture I'd missed due to the sick cat issue. I'd have to call back tomorrow during office hours, which was fine. Any time the DA called, I got worry lines. They were the state agency that oversaw and inspected shelters. I'd never had any issue passing those surprise inspections. The fact they were calling me was what had me nervously chewing the inside of my lower lip. They said they'd emailed me, and actually when I went looking, it was just a survey. Still, my heart was still racing in my chest.

"Hey, man, are you okay? Get some bad nachos or something?"

The sound of eighteen thousand fans reappeared around me. I shook off the cloud of worry and turned to Mr. Mountain—who I now knew had a real name, Kenny—and smiled up at the huge season-ticket holder. Seemed Max had sprung for these seats throughout the rest of the playoffs. Color me surprised. That man was full of lovely little secrets.

"Nope, no bad nachos. Just thinking about work."

"Dude, don't you know the rule?" Kenny gave his husband, Jeff, a look. Jeff glanced around his bare-chested spouse. "Baby, he don't know the rule."

"Sorry? What rule is that?" I asked.

Someone on the ice hit someone else on the ice, and the fans shouted obscenities. Dammit. I needed to pay attention to the game. That could have been Max getting knocked into the boards instead of Adler. Not that I wanted Adler to get his bell rung, but you know…

"The rule that states work stays in the parking lot at a hockey game."

"Oh, right, that rule. I forgot."

Kenny patted my head, then went back to roaring at Tampa Bay for some infraction or another. This second game had been downright brutal so far. We were almost at the end of the second period with things all tied up. There had been no scoring because the teams had been too busy hitting each other. Between the legal and illegal checks, the sin bin had needed a revolving door. I suspected the Railers were in for a good chewing-out when they returned to the dressing room.

My attention seemed to be on Max most of the time, but I did get to enjoy a sudden flurry of activity around the Florida net just as the horn blew signaling the end of the period. That was the most offense the Railers had been able to muster throughout forty minutes of play. Hopefully they'd be able to keep that jazzy goodness going when they came back out.

"I'm going to the bathroom and grabbing a beer. Kenny, Jeff, you want something?"

"No, we're good. Thanks, though." Kenny beamed at me, his arm dangling around his husband's neck. Jeff smiled softly. Talk about an odd couple, but they seemed to be happy.

I joined the mass exodus of fans heading to the concourse for food, drink, and a potty run.

Progress was slow, one step at a time, which gave me plenty of time to look around.

People of all sizes and shapes and colors were there. Lots of kids and women too. I was glad to see that. I'll cop to being the only hockey fan among my group of friends back home. Most were into basketball or football. I liked those sports too, but there had always been something about hockey that I loved. The speed and the physicality and the grace of the big men on those thin blades. Maybe someday I could con Max into giving me a few skating lessons.

A tall man in front of me left the queue. I stepped

up and glanced to the side and saw Rolf leaning on the thick railing. My foot missed the next step, and I stumbled into a woman.

"Excuse me," I mumbled to her dirty glare. My sight flew back to the next section, and he was still there, his gaze never moving from me. Heart in my chest, I pawed in my back pocket to find my phone. Hands shaking, I dialed 9-1-1, feeling less terrified with every ring. When the dispatcher answered, I threw a look at the exact place Rolf had been glowering at me and found only a railing. No. Shit. Where did he go?

"Hello? What is your emergency?" the dispatcher asked.

"I... He was here. My brother-in-law. Ex. He was — Shit, where did he go?!"

"Sir, I need you to calm down and tell me the nature of your emergency."

"Rolf. He was here. I mean..." I rubbed at my sweaty brow. "He was right there." I pointed at the railing overlooking the bowl of seats down below, as if the woman on the other end of the call could see where I was pointing. "I mean...it looked just like him."

"Sir, can you please tell me the nature of your emergency?"

"I ah... Sorry, I think I overreacted. Sorry for calling. Sorry." I ended the call, heart hammering inside my rib cage. It had been him. Right? Same blond hair, same icy blue eyes, same hateful expression. It had to have been him. Did I imagine it?

"Sweet Lord," I groaned. I turned and went back to my seat.

"Thought you were grabbing a piss and a beer," Kenny said when I dropped down beside him.

"Too many people," I replied, my gaze now touching on every golden head in the stands. Had Rolf followed me here? Had he been lurking around the shelter? My house? Or was I losing my mind?

Badly rattled, I stayed right beside Kenny the Mountain until the Railers managed to lose by one sneaky wraparound goal. I exited with Kenny and Jeff, then lured them into staying with me by offering them the chance to meet Max outside. They were all kinds of up for that, so I hid behind my new friends and waited outside in the dark for Max to come out and give me the hug I so badly needed. Maybe he could kick my ass as well, for being such a damn silly fool.

Chapter Twelve

Max

Something changed. I don't know what it was specifically, but when I saw Ben next, he wouldn't look me in the eye.

I'd seen this before in guys I'd had fuck-buddy status with. We were guys, and we weren't going to sit down and have some fucking heart-to-heart about our feelings. So you start to avoid the guy, act as though he doesn't exist, and then finally he gets the message and moves on with no hard feelings.

Just as Ben was doing.

He was distracted, wouldn't look me in the eyes, as I said, and when we were together the night before he'd gone to bed citing a headache, leaving me in his front room staring at the TV showing reruns of *Friends*.

Maybe I should get the hint already. Ben was clearly doing that guy thing, and I should move on to concentrating on what was important—hockey.

Only, it wasn't what I wanted to do, and people didn't call me a stubborn asshole for nothing. After ten minutes of angsting about the message I was being given, I decided I was ready to give a message of my own. He was nothing but a lump under the covers, no sign of any part of him, and I stood for a while at the bedroom door and stared at the shape of him. I just wanted to be sure to say exactly the right thing. Something like "don't go", or "don't leave me". He moved under the covers, and I stiffened. I wasn't ready to talk to him yet because I didn't have the right words.

I was still stuck in that loop of how much of myself I had to give. The doctor wanted to see me, said I was not handling things as he expected me to. Well, fuck him, I was handling everything okay. You ask any man with a ticking time bomb in his head how he's handling shit, and we'll all say the same thing.

A day at a time. Every day is a win.

I backed away from the door and went back into Ben's small kitchen, taking a stool and staring at my phone. The last three non-Ben calls had been to Doctor Warner. He was probably used to me calling by now with my stupid worries. The last call had ended with a very uncharacteristic "you need to calm down" from Doc, but then I had phoned him at four a.m. his time, and let's face it, he isn't a twenty-four-hour on-call guy. He's a renowned neurosurgeon.

If we made it to become one of the two teams in the finals of the Stanley Cup, then at the most, seven games were all that remained between us and the cup. That would take me into next month, which was only another three weeks.

What were the chances of my head thing getting the better of me in that time?

I shouldn't worry.

Yeah, right, who am I kidding? Worry happens without me controlling it.

Right here, in this kitchen, in the soft glow of a small lamp, I was the very definition of someone scared for tomorrow.

What if the worst-case scenario played out? What if I collapsed and no one knew why? What if I got into a fight and a fist made contact with my head at just the right angle to cause a bleed? Hell, what if I went to bed and didn't wake up?

I felt utterly lonely and vulnerable, and it was all because of one man and his inability to look me in the eyes.

"What's wrong?" Ben said behind me. He sounded sleepy.

I shrugged. I wasn't going to turn and face him, because I knew I wouldn't be able to face seeing his expression and knowing he wanted me to leave. He hugged me from behind, and I stared down at his hands against my shirt. Unbidden, my own covered his. If this meant everything was over, then I wanted one last touch.

Sap.

"Sorry I've been distracted," he murmured against my skin, and I couldn't help the skip of my heart at his words. "Just a lot on my mind."

I turned on the seat and faced him, and he cupped my face with his hands, pressing a soft kiss to my lips.

"Sometimes…" he began softly and stopped.

"Sometimes what?" I prompted, because he looked so serious.

He sighed, and I took that to mean he didn't want to say anything else, but I was wrong.

"I think my mind is playing tricks with me. I thought I saw Rolf at the last game, and then yesterday I could have sworn I saw him outside the house, but when I went outside it wasn't him." He huffed a soft laugh. "I think I need my head tested."

At that point, I could have said something. That was the perfect segue into me and my issues. I could have just said, hey, Ben, I've had this thing in my head that has a name too long and complicated to pronounce, but hey, it's okay, the doc says it's unlikely to happen again, but you never know, because there is a ten percent chance that it might. I could die next time. Are you okay with that?

I didn't say a damn thing.

Coward.

Instead I turned the whole thing back onto him with my addiction to worrying about him.

"What if it was him?"

He shook his head and kissed me again, trying to distract me, no doubt. "Yeah, he just happened to get a ticket to a Railers game that was sold out when he doesn't even like hockey. Believe me, I know I'm losing my shit. The cops warned him—what else can we do? It's DK I worry about, poor kid."

I stood up and hugged him close. "I worry about you," I admitted.

Now. Tell him about your own fears now, in the semi-darkness, where it's safe.

I opened my mouth to talk, and he kissed the words away.

"Come to bed," he murmured.

I switched the lamp off and followed him to the bedroom. When I got there, he was already under the covers, holding them up to his chin and smiling up at me. I didn't feel the need to jump his bones—I wanted to stare at his gorgeous face, hold him close, and just love him as hard as I could.

Yeah.

I think I could love Ben.

. . .

WHEN WE WOKE, it was to the brightest and warmest of early summer days. DK was opening the shelter that morning, taking on more responsibility, which Ben was encouraging. That meant a lazy morning for my man, if lazy meant not getting out of bed until eight and eating breakfast together. He was still going to work at nine, but we managed to fit in a whole lot of kisses and smiles before we left the house.

My Uber was waiting for me, and Ben shook his head.

"So tacky," he teased. "Get your own car, Mr. Millionaire."

"I don't drive," I said, probably way more defensive than I needed to be at that point. He shot me a look of confusion at the tone, but I kissed away his frown.

We parted after that kiss and a hug and went in our opposite directions. I was early for skate, but I needed to work on conditioning and talk to the PT about the nagging pain in my knee. Damn thing had this way of spasming at all the wrong times.

By the time I was dressed and out on the ice for practice skate, I'd been pummeled and iced and was in my happy place. The skate itself was more about loosening muscles than strategy; we'd got this far, one game away from winning the conference and advancing to the Cup fight, and we were exhausted and energized at the same time.

The mood was good. We had the number of the

team we were facing, and tomorrow night, right here on home ice, we could take this.

Jared gestured me over, and along with the rest of the D, we circled him as he talked strategy. We were a sight to behold, me towering over the rest, some of us were two-way D-men, able to take the fight to the net, others, like me, able to change the direction of a game on a single fight. Together we were a brick wall, and when Stan ambled up to stand with us, I couldn't help myself. I tugged him into a head-hold and kissed his helmet.

He muttered something in Russian I had no hope in hell of understanding, but it didn't sound like a curse, more a soft noise of affection.

This was my team.

And we were going to win tomorrow, and we were going to the finals. I could feel it in my bones.

Winning wasn't easy, though. Tied after three periods, we were battling to the wire, but when we pulled that final goal, Ten and his magic on a break-away, assisting a beautiful goal from Dieter, I'd never felt anything like it before.

Ecstasy, exhaustion, love, passion, fear…hell, this was a complete and utter meltdown of my emotions. I looked for Ben in the stands, saw him standing and clapping and cheering, and I blew him a kiss. He made a show of catching it and holding it to his heart. Toly caught me in a hug, pulling me around and into the huddle of men burying Stan on the ice. Ten whooped in my ear, and I was grinning like the Cheshire Cat. I knew it.

"We're going to the Stanley Cup Final!" someone yelled. Or at least I caught the words "Stanley Cup" and "going"; other than that, the cacophony of noises was too much to bear.

Connor skated over as captain, Troy Larsen and Toly as the alternates by his side, none of them touching the cup we'd won as top dogs in the Eastern Conference. Skaters and their superstitions meant no team touched that cup. Unless it was a team who'd found luck after touching it; I'd seen that as well. Hell, I can't explain what represents luck to someone. All I knew was that my luck was in the crowd shouting for our team, and for me.

The mood in the locker room was euphoric, and all the talk was about the West Coast team we would be meeting to fight for the Stanley Cup. The Raptors would win their games on the West Coast; they were the higher rated in the first three rounds and had more regular-season points than us. That meant our first Cup final games would be on their ice, but none of us cared at that moment about the home-ice advantage they would have.

The Railers were team-killers.

We could beat *anyone.*

My energy left me after a few minutes of hugs and back-patting, and I sagged onto my small part of the bench, still grinning but unable to contain the exhaustion from the game.

Toly slumped next to me, and we knocked shoulders.

"Fucking worth it," I said.

Toly snorted a laugh. "So worth it."

THE HIGH LASTED through post-game interviews, showers, getting dressed, and all the way until I saw Ben waiting for me, DK at his side. I hugged Ben so close I doubted he could breathe until, laughing, he pushed me away.

"Get a room." DK smirked, and I pulled him in for a hug, giving him a noogie and holding him still even as he fought me.

I felt strong enough to take on the whole damn world.

We made it back to Ben's without discussing where we'd be going. I loved his place; small but warm, it was the direct opposite of my temporary place in the apartment block. His house was home and family, all wrapped up in cozy furniture and his big-screen TV. We dropped DK off on the way, and then it was just us at his place, drinking each other in and loving so hard.

Wrapped in his arms afterward, I knew I had to tell him about the worries I was keeping inside.

Without sharing that last part of me, I wouldn't be able to live with myself anymore.

"I need to tell you something," I began, and extricated myself from his hold, sitting up in the bed and tucking the quilt around me. He scooted up next to me and gripped my hand.

"Me too," he said.

We could do that whole "you first" thing, but hell, I needed to clear the air of my secrets.

"I'll go first," I said, and he smiled at me like he was waiting for me to tell him the most wonderful thing in the world.

"Go on, then," he encouraged when I didn't talk straight away.

"Just after I was traded, I had a medical thing."

He poked me, then, "I can understand longer words than 'thing'."

He didn't sound pissed or worried, but then I hadn't told him everything.

"It was an arteriovenous malformation, an AVM." I waited for him to show some understanding, quietly hoping I wouldn't have to explain, but he looked blank.

"What is that?"

"A blockage of sorts that causes bleeds on the brain, can cause strokes, that kind of thing. I had an operation to remove the blockage, completely successful." I added the last bit in a careless way, as if it wasn't vital he took those words as the most important.

"Shit." Now he was worried, concerned, holding my hand and looking at me with those sexy liquid-chocolate eyes. "I'm so sorry, that must have been so scary."

"It is."

At first I didn't realize what I'd said. I was soft and sated from making love, and Ben was holding my hand; I couldn't even think that those two small words could mark the beginning of the end.

"What do you mean, 'it is'?" Ben untangled his fingers from mine. "You mean it *was* scary. Right? It's done now?"

It wasn't as if I was going to hold back the worries I had now, but the way he stressed that word made me reconsider how honest I was going to be. I wouldn't share my fears, just the cold medical facts.

"Well, I still see a specialist in case it comes back."

"Back."

Was Ben going to repeat everything I said?

"Well, yeah, there's a chance there may be another blockage at some time, but I'm used to living with that now." No sense in giving him the statistics that haunted me.

I saw him move. Just a little. A few inches away from me. His expression changed from sympathetic to this blank nothing I couldn't get a handle on at all. I reached for his hand, but he avoided my touch.

"Ben?"

He stared right at me, and then in a smooth movement he slid out of bed and yanked on his jeans and a T-shirt.

"You're dying?" He said dully.

"No, not if I have anything to do with it."

"You could die and you didn't tell me."

"Ben—"

"I can't do this again. You need to leave," he said. His tone was dead.

"Don't be stupid, Ben. Let's talk some more," I said with a smile. He didn't let me say anything else, so I didn't get to say anything about how I was living with it, and so should he now if he really cared.

"I don't care—get out of my house."

I scrambled to stand, feeling at a disadvantage naked, pulling on my underwear and post-game suit, desperately trying to find the words to get him to calm the fuck down.

"Ben, come on."

He stalked out of the bedroom, and I followed him. He had my shoes in his hands, and he opened the front door and threw them out on the step.

"Get out," he shouted.

"You're being stupid."

I looked at my shoes lying outside, only knowing this was an overreaction. What right did he have to know everything about me? I kept things to myself. This was my life. Not his.

"Fuck you," he snapped, and I blinked at him. "You lied to me."

Anger poked at me, and I pulled on my jacket. "I wasn't lying. This isn't something I share with anyone—"

"I'm not just anyone!"

"I didn't know I could trust you not to tell the team—"

"You want to know what I was going to say to you tonight?" Ben interrupted, and he jerked back from the door so I could go through. "I was going to tell you I loved you."

"Jesus, Ben—"

His lips twisted into the parody of a smile. "Good job you got there first with your secrets."

"Ben, you're not making any sense."

"Get out." This time there was no anger, more regret and a finality that bit at me.

I love you too.

I stepped outside and picked up my shoes, turned back to get him to calm down, but he slammed the door on me.

"You're the only person I've ever told," I said to the door. He was being an asshole now, throwing a man out in the dead of night. A man who had no car.

The door opened and hope bloomed in my chest, but all that happened was Ben threw out my phone, which I managed to catch. The door was shut before I could say a thing.

I wanted to take back all the words. Why had I thought sharing my fears would be a good thing?

No one cared about me or my worries. I was pretty much alone in the world, and that was how I liked it.

By the time I'd reached the sidewalk and turned right to find a space where I could call a cab that wasn't right outside Ben's place, I was over Ben and his overreaction.

The best sex I'd ever had wasn't enough for me to be with someone like him.

Fuck him.

Chapter Thirteen

Ben

"Benton Isaiah Worthington!"

I cringed as my name echoed down the still quiet street. I'd thought I'd get away from my aunts by running before six in the morning.

"Why did you make crafty old women go to bed early and get up even earlier?" I asked God as I slowly turned to face Aunt Glenna storming down her walk. God was quiet. He had been for the past week. Wished I could say the same for my great-aunts and nephew.

"Are you running again?" She stopped right in front of me, sharp brown eyes moving up from my running shoes to my running shorts to my old, ripped Washington running T-shirt.

"Nope, I'm off to paint a mural."

"Do not get wise-mouthed with me, young man. I can still whip your backside with no help from the Lord," Aunt Glenna snapped, a finger waving under my nose.

"Sorry, ma'am."

"Mmm, you had better be. You know you can't run away from being a damn fool."

I closed my eyes and drew in a deep lungful of city air.

Sweet Baby Jesus, can you please get my family off my back about Max? I've truly heard enough. Can the old gals be struck mute? Just maybe for a week or two? To let me get back on my feet and try to repair my broken heart. Amen.

"Did you want me for something other than calling me a damn fool?"

"Someone has to point out what a damn fool you are."

I rolled my eyes to the heavens.

Anyone up there listening?

No booming voice from the clear sky to be heard. Just dogs and traffic.

"Okay, well, you're two up on Carol for the day. Did you want something?" I folded my arms over my tattered Washington shirt, eager to be off.

"I need you to buy me Band-Aids." She dug in her robe, way down where her boobs would be, and pulled out two one-dollar bills.

"Band-Aids. Why do you need Band-Aids at six in

the morning?" I refused to take the boob money when she tried to push it into my hand.

"Maybe I cut myself."

Right. Good. This I needed right now? No, I did not. "I was planning on going the other direction. Are you losing a lot of blood? I know how to make a tourniquet."

"Do not get smart with me, Benton. I'm going to shave my legs. It's been since winter and I want to wear shorts to the voters' rights rally on the weekend."

"Dear Lord." I sighed, the thought of her hairy legs and where the hell she'd had those bills hidden spurring me to get moving. Those kinds of thoughts needed to be expunged ASAP. "Fine, I'll go the opposite direction of where I was planning to so I can stop at Mike's Drugstore and buy you Band-Aids. I'd hate to see you bleed out from a wound inflicted by one of those pink lady razors."

She nodded. "Guess you're not a total damn fool. It's always wise to do what your elders tell you to do."

With that, she took her boob money and pattered back to her house, stopping to yell at someone going too fast down the street.

"Lord, give me strength."

I went south instead of north, falling into the pace of a nice run. I'd thought of bringing Bucky, but it was already too hot for a dog from the North. He hadn't been happy to go back into his crate, but I was trying to be a good dog dad. He was the only thing I had in my life. Again.

Why had he lied to me? Fucking Max. Why? When he'd had all that time and he knew—he *knew*—how terrible it had been for me to lose Liam. That bastard had sat there and listened to me talk about the agony of loss, how I'd wanted to die from the sheer misery of losing the man I loved. He'd laid beside me, held me, told me shit to placate me, made me fall in love with him, and all that time he'd had this thing in his head. This thing that could take him from me without warning. And he'd never said a word. Not once.

I had to stop at the corner to dash away sweat and tears from my eyes. I lingered there, shaking out my hands, pacing, trying to push down the anger and pain of that deceit.

Traffic stopped. I jogged across the intersection, soaked with sweat, unable to let the joy of exercise wipe away Max. Nothing was helping. Not running or work. Max lingered everywhere, around every corner, in each room of my house. His smell was on my bedding, his razor and toothbrush on my counter, and some of his clothes were still in my hamper.

Four blocks later, I slowed and stretched outside Mike's Drugstore I hoped I wasn't too smelly to shop. Just in case, I made a fast pass through the store, which had just opened, so there were hardly any customers, to grab a box of Band-Aids. While I was there, I made a pass through the hair care aisle, grabbing a bottle of intensive hydrating shampoo and conditioner. Honey-berry scent, my favorite. I had used the last of my shampoo yesterday. Shampooing daily wasn't good for my hair—I usually only washed it once a week and then conditioned the hell out of it with some deep-conditioning hair tonic—but the daily runs meant I had to shampoo in the shower. I mean I *had* to. To hell with the dry hair worry, my head felt gross after a run.

Waiting in line for the register to open, praying I didn't smell like stinky man, I thought back to the morning Max had used my shampoo and conditioner. His hair had laid flat on his head, slick and kind of greasy despite several rinses.

"You might want to sort your hair out," I teased, then rolled him back into bed for a nice long kiss and cuddle session. The memory of that tender moment pierced me like a lance.

It took forever to get rung up. Stepping out of the cool of that pharmacy into the heat of a city summer day stole my breath. Or maybe I was still gasping after being gutted by that memory of better days. I glanced across the street, and there sat the Rose of Beulah Baptist Church.

My phone buzzed in the back pocket of my shorts. Pulling it out, suspecting it was an aunt with another pharmacy-related need, I nearly dropped the phone when I saw it was a text from Max. It had been ten days since we'd spoken. The Railers and Raptors had each won a game. I hadn't watched, DK had. I couldn't look at Max on TV and be calm, cool, and collected. DK was furious I wouldn't tell him what had happened to break us up. Which put him in company with my aunts and most of my employees.

I'm so fucking stupid

I re-read it a couple of times, hoping context about what he meant would magically appear. Did he mean he was stupid to have slept with me? Was he texting me to start an argument? What kind of text was that to send me? My thumb hovered over delete, and another text flashed up before I could.

I've been missing you

"I've been missing you too," I murmured, sweat slipping into my eye and making it water.

I didn't know if I should reply or not. I hated the man. Didn't I? Well, maybe hate was too strong. I was mad at him, though. So damn mad. Livid. Angry as hell for how he had uncaringly omitted something that important from any dialog we'd ever had. All the openings he'd had, and he'd never once said jack shit. That hurt on a cellular level. I just could not grasp how you could sleep with someone, eat at their table, make love to them, ride in Kissing Towers with them, yet not have the common decency to say, "Hey, Ben, I got this thing in my head and it might come back and kill me. Just thought you should know before you fall head-over-heels in love with my stupid-ass face."

I did love his stupid-ass face, though. And his smile, and the way he made me laugh and made me cry out in passion. I even loved how he thought he knew what good dancing was, when he obviously didn't. I spun around, looking for a direction to go in or a sign. Something that would guide me, because I was about as confused and frightened as a man could be. My soul ached. A sharp, shooting pain ripped through my side. I groaned and winced in such agony —memory or cramp, it was hard to discern—that I slapped a hand to my side and shuffled across the street when there was a gap in traffic. Maybe a break in the shadowy interior of my church would ease my mind.

The house of worship's doors were open, as they always were come five a.m. It was dark inside, cool, the smell of lemon wax rising from the newly polished pews. It was funny, but every time I smelled lemon furniture polish, I thought of God.

Side still caught in a spasm, I dropped into the closest pew, breathless and lost and scared beyond reason, Max's text still unanswered. I used the hem of my shirt to dry my face after placing the bag from the drugstore on the pew beside me. Once my face was dry, I studied the pulpit way up front. The wood was rich oak. On each side of the pulpit were stands to hold flowers. They were empty today but come Sunday they'd be filled with glorious color. Behind the flowers and pulpit was a large wooden cross, dark brown, as old as my great-aunts. I sat there for the longest time, staring at the cross, whispering for God to help guide me from this mess my life was in. If he couldn't offer guidance, how about just a signpost or an answer?

"Ben, did you get your a.m. and p.m. mixed up?" Pastor Bert asked from the front of the church. "Choir practice is at seven at *night*."

He smiled widely as he walked past his pulpit and up the aisle.

"No, sir, I was just in need of some counsel."

"Ah, well, the Lord is who I turn to when I'm lost."

I sighed. "He's not saying much."

"I have found he's the silent type. Perhaps you could tell me what's troubling you?"

I glanced at my pastor, then back at the cross. "How much do you know?"

"Well, I know you and Max have run into some difficulty, but what that difficulty is has been hard to pry out of you. Although your aunts have told me enough."

That made me smile a bit. "They do like to talk."

"They're concerned about you. But yes, they do like to talk." He chuckled and wiggled back into the pew, making the wood squeak.

"I want this to stay between us," I opened.

"Of course."

He patted my sweaty back, and I started talking.

Guess I shouldn't have made fun of my aunts' love of gabbing. I talked and talked and talked, and Pastor Bert listened. When I was out of words, I closed my eyes and slithered back into the pew, mentally and physically exhausted.

"It sounds to me as if both you and Max are caught up in fear."

"He lied to me."

"Because he was afraid. And you threw him out because you're afraid of losing another man you love."

Head resting on the back of the pew, I opened my eyes and stared at the smooth white ceiling.

"I can't do that again, Pastor. I cannot give my all to a man then for him to die. I just…I can't." Tears ran down my cheeks and into my ears.

"I know facing those fears is hard. But don't give in to them. If you do, you won't be able to talk to your heart."

I rolled my head to the left to gaze on the man of God. "Was that from the Bible?" My scripture knowledge was pretty slack .

Pastor Bert smiled. "No, it's a favored quote of mine from Paulo Coelho, but don't tell God I'm not using his word for counseling one of my sheep. He might fire me."

That made me laugh. Out loud.

"You think Max is my heart?" I asked, using the backs of my hands to dry my face.

"Do *you* think Max is your heart?"

I nodded and sat up straight.

"Then you'll need to push your fear aside so you can hear what your heart has to say."

That made sense. I was terrified to reply to that text, though.

"Thank you," I said as Pastor Bert pushed to his feet.

He placed his hand on my shoulder and smiled. "If you need me, I'll be back in my office, having coffee."

He ambled off, humming a song that sounded a great deal like Prince's "Raspberry Beret".

I drew in a long, deep breath, pulled out my phone, and sent Max a text in return.

I've been missing you too.

It took a moment for him to reply.

Can we talk?

I wanted to weep, laugh, and vomit. Love was one confusing emotion.

I'd like that. Tonight, at the shelter after closing. Six?

I knew there was no game tonight. That would be tomorrow night. Sitting there with that phone in my hand, trembling with nerves and fear and excitement, I waited to see if he'd come and talk with me. Maybe…. just maybe… we could both conquer our fears and listen to our hearts.

See you at six. I'm sorry. I suck at this love shit.

I swallowed down a sickly laugh/sob because God

had probably heard enough of my sniffling for one damn morning. Thumbs moving slowly because nerves and giddiness had taken over my central nervous system, I tapped out the only reply that came to mind.

I'm sorry too. I suck as well. Let's suck together.

Max hit me back with a wink emoji I didn't understand until I read my previous text over and blushed clear to my toes.

"Sorry God. I didn't mean that to be as dirty as it sounded." I slid out of the pew and out into the heat before the Rose of Beulah Baptist Church was struck by a mysterious thunderbolt.

Chapter Fourteen

Max

"And?" Toly asked me pointedly as he knocked my socked foot with his own.

I looked up from my phone at the men ranged in front of me. Connor was worried, Ten looked all kinds of serious, Stan stood with his arms across his chest in his best version of intimidating. And Toly? He was sitting next to me as if he thought I needed the support.

I do need support.

I'd fucked everything up. When I left Ben's house, I was determined to forget him, assign him to the group of people I'd met, fucked, and then left. He wasn't going to be important to me. I didn't need him, or his complicated reasoning about why he now hated me. So his husband had died. What did that have to do with me? I'd lied, or at least omitted the entire brain thing, but that didn't make a difference to a sex life. Right? What was his problem?

Whatever I'd done, whoever I was, in that moment, I was over Ben.

Then when I woke up the next day, the regret began.

At first it was nothing more than a subtle push and a need to find someone to talk to. Who did I choose? I was new here, and I'd already decided I wasn't sharing this at the rink. Until, of course, I fucked up in the second game of the Stanley Cup final series against the Raptors, played like a robot, got into three fights, and spent most of my time in the bin. We lost that one, and even though we'd won the first game, we weren't ahead anymore.

The team had an intervention, and they hadn't left me alone since then. Which led to the texting, because we're a group of guys and the concept of face-to-face talking about our feelings wasn't one we liked the idea of.

"We're meeting up tonight," I summarized. Ten high-fived Stan, Connor sighed dramatically, and Toly bumped elbows with me.

"Thank fuck for that," Connor muttered. After all, he was the captain and I had fucked up in the last game. I was lucky I wasn't benched.

"And what are you going to say to Ben?" Toly said. He wasn't actually asking me that. No, he wanted me to confirm I'd understood what he'd *told* me to say.

None of them knew about the reason it had all gone wrong. I'd simply told them I'd fucked up. I knew it was all on me. Of course, Ben would be afraid; of course he would worry. None of this was his fault.

"I'm going to say sorry for fucking up and beg him for a second chance."

"Too damn right," Toly muttered.

A commotion outside the circle had the guys parting, and Adler pushed right in.

"So, is this knitting circle just for you, or can anyone join in?"

Adler was just what we needed, because we exchanged smiles and then everyone scattered.

Adler wrinkled his nose. "What did I miss?"

"Men problems," I said honestly.

Adler nodded like he knew exactly what I was talking about. "I know what you mean. You know Layton shouted at me for not putting the lid back on the coffee?" He huffed as if that was the worst thing in the world. And maybe for Adler it was the worst thing. But for me? I wished my problems were as small as that.

I was next up for PT. My right knee was still giving me problems. Nothing I couldn't handle, but it made me feel every one of my thirty years. I was a veteran, and my body was used up. At least when I was being poked, prodded and pushed around I could clear my head and think about the things I wanted to say to Ben.

I put a call in to Doctor Warner as soon as I was back in my apartment, drinking coffee and listening to him telling me the statistics, the worries, the concerns, and the fact that maybe I'd been concentrating on the negatives more than the positives.

Armed with information, I headed to the shelter and to Ben, asking the cab driver to drop me around the corner. He'd recognized me. That happened sometimes, though rarely—being Max van Hellren wasn't the same as being Tennant Rowe. I needed some time to get my head straight after talking for fifteen minutes about the Cup run, and I leaned against the wall. I watched a car slow down as it rounded the corner, recognized one of the security team I'd hired on his half-hourly drive-by. He nodded at me, and all I did was give a half wave. People were looking out for the man I loved, and I was reassured.

Ben will understand. Ben will forgive me. I love Ben.

I repeated the words over and over, and finally I was ready to face the music, at five fifty-seven exactly.

He was waiting for me, side gate open, and security cameras be damned, I pulled him into my arms and held him close.

"I'm sorry," I said against his neck. He eased me back and away, then kissed me. Not hard, not dangerously, but softly, whispering words between kisses that I couldn't even hear.

Then it was my turn to ease him away.

"We need to talk," I said.

He grasped my hand and tugged me away from the gate, pulling it closed and leading me into the office area. The place was quiet apart from soft snuffling noises from the puppies as they slept. We checked in on them. Ben made coffee, and we didn't talk, not until we were in his office, on his ratty sofa, and turned to face each other.

"I'm sorry—"

"I wanted to say—"

We began to talk at the same time and ended up grinning at each other.

"You first," I encouraged.

"I love you," he began plainly. "I don't want to lose you."

"I don't want to lose you either."

"I'm not the one with a broken head," he said, and smiled wryly.

"I talked to my doctor again today, asked him again for the stats, and the possibilities, and the probabilities. Before, I focused so much on the negative I never listened to the parts where he said I might never have a problem again. But..." I had to be honest. "There is a chance I'll have another bleed, and that could be a stroke, or my heart could stop, or shit, the list of horrors is a long one."

He studied me carefully. "Hockey doesn't help, does it?"

That was it. The crux of the matter. The danger I put myself in every time I went out on the ice. It was an acceptable risk for doing what I loved. Hell, I would say the adrenaline of fighting was enough to get me back on the ice each time. But now? The risk wasn't acceptable, because I had something to fight for.

"Hockey is everything to me," I began. I'd rehearsed this part to the last word. "I was three when I strapped on my first skates, held my first stick. It was in my blood, and the focus of my entire life was to get to the NHL. I'm good. Better than good—I was born to skate." He reached over and took my hand and held it as I tried to make him see why I had made the decision I had. "And at the top of that is the Cup. It's something that's defined my life. Five more games, maybe only three, and I could have that one shining thing. I can't let my team down. I can't take myself away from hockey. But then I met you, and now you're so important to me."

I stopped and dropped my gaze. I couldn't look at the emotion in his dark eyes and not feel choked up. I was admitting that even though I had feelings for him, *loved him*, I had to finish the other part of my life before I could have a life with him

He squeezed my hand, and I looked up at him.

He didn't look angry, or resigned—if anything, there was understanding in his expression.

"Don't hate me," I pleaded.

"I love you," Ben repeated. Then he lifted my hand to his lips and pressed a kiss to my scarred knuckles. That kiss meant something. Maybe it was a promise, but it was a gift he was giving me.

"Maximum five more games, and then I'm done."

"Then what will you do?"

I leaned in to him and kissed him, just as gently as he had kissed me. "Then I'll spend the rest of my life working out the best ways of loving you every day."

He kissed me back then, and somehow I knew we'd found a middle ground to work from. What more could a thirty-year-old wrecked man want from the man he had fallen for?

At first the cacophonous noises that pierced the silence of our kisses meant nothing, and then Ben was shoving me away, and I stood up maybe a moment later, following Ben, who sprinted out of the office. I smelled it before we reached it. Fire.

"Call 9-1-1!" Ben shouted back over his shoulder, and I scrabbled for my cell, connecting and reporting the fire even as Ben disappeared into the smoke.

The puppies.

I didn't even think, I followed Ben and found him scooping the puppies out of their pen, trying to corral them even as they thought he was playing. He handed me three.

"One of the pens outside," he ordered, and I did what he said, sprinting as fast as I could to the outside pens, finding the nearest empty one and pushing the puppies inside. He was right behind me, carrying four, and then with the two of us going back in we rescued the remaining pups, shut the door to try to stop the fire spreading, and turned our attention to whatever hell we had to deal with next. The fire was hot, contained at the moment in the office building, but the first kennel and storage weren't far beyond, and if the fire leaped between? I grabbed the office extinguisher, and aimed it at the flames, standing between them and the kennels. As if I could stop the fire just by being there.

I had to stop the flames from reaching the Cat House. God knew Ben would dive into the fire to save his animals.

I exhausted the contents. Maybe it slowed the flames, maybe it didn't—I couldn't fucking tell. Ben was struggling under the weight of a huge mastiff, and I helped him. He was emptying the kennels in danger and moving dogs down, but what if the fire caught the kennels and spread?

Then I saw him.

Saw them.

At the same time as Ben, who froze next to me.

Rolf was there, DK standing in front of him with his hands raised and his face bloody. I stepped forward again, putting myself between Ben and Rolf, whose lips were pulled back in a snarl.

"DK?" I heard Ben say.

"I'm sorry, Ben, he made me—"

"Let it burn," Rolf said, and shoved DK forward. "Let it all burn."

He pushed DK again, and the kid stumbled into me.

"All of you back into the office."

Behind us, the fire was crackling, ceilings caving. He wanted us back in the fire. None of us were doing that.

He waved a gun in our direction and in the light of the fire his eyes held a crazed look. "Into the fucking offices. All of you can burn."

Ben took a step back away from me; I could see him in my peripheral vision. What was he doing?

I moved again, making sure it was me right in front of Ben and DK. I was bigger, and a gun didn't scare me. Nothing scared me when I was in the moment.

"Move!" Rolf screamed. He stepped toward me, and I didn't even think. I wasn't going to stand there and let things happen to me, to *us*, so I staggered forward, used my entire body weight to tackle the bastard to the ground, and he went as easily as a rookie on new skates. I pinned him, the gun between us, and I fought for that gun, gripping and scraping and scratching at every bit of bare skin, ignoring every curse from Rolf.

No one threatened what I loved.

He was surprisingly strong, bucking up under me, and at one point he got the gun free, waving it wildly. I slammed his hand to the ground, hearing his scream and the discharge of the gun. I pulled the thing loose and moved away, picking up the gun as I rolled and coming to a kneel pointing the gun right at him.

"Stay there, fucker," I shouted over the noise of the fire and the sirens.

Thank fuck for the sirens.

I glanced over at Ben, who was kneeling on the floor, holding his arm, DK trying to help him stand, and then the chaos increased.

Someone took the gun from me, another person helped me stand, asked me what had happened, but all that time I was staring at Ben and the blood on his white shirt. He'd been hurt.

I pushed my way to him, ignored people calling after me.

"What happened?"

"The bullet scraped him," DK explained even as I shoved my way closer to Ben. The gun? A bullet? I'd done this to him. Regrets were sour in my mouth, and then he did this incredible thing. He simply smiled.

"Thank you," he said.

"I shot you," I said blindly.

"Rolf shot me—he was the one with the gun."

"Are you... Can I..." I'd lost the ability to talk, and then it was too late, the firefighter in charge talking to Ben, volunteers there the dogs, and abruptly I was standing on my own by the gate.

"We have him on camera," someone said at my side.

I rounded on him, the same man I'd seen in the car on the drive-by. I wanted to shake him. How had Rolf gotten past him?

He held up a hand as if he knew what I was going to say. "We saw the gun on the owner's nephew, called in backup."

I couldn't listen to this, to any of it, and I went to find Ben.

Finding him with the dogs, talking to a visibly shaken DK, I hugged him from behind.

"What can I do?"

He turned in my hold, and his eyes held shadows. "I don't know where to start."

"You should go to the hospital," I heard myself say, but I knew he wouldn't do that.

"I need to make sure... The dogs..."

"The dogs and cats are fine." I glanced at his arm, the widening red patch on his sleeve and the slick patch of wet blood on his forearm.

"I'll go later."

"*Ben.*"

"I swear I'll go later. It's just a scratch."

Damn scratch sure was bleeding. I stopped

arguing with him, though. I did make DK find a first aid kit and tend to his uncle while I assisted in whatever way I could.

I stayed with him and helped him, hated the worry in his eyes, watching as shock made him clumsy, knowing the strain on his shoulders, and I didn't think about hockey once.

OF COURSE, that came back to bite me in the ass come morning. I'd been up most of the night, working with Ben, finally giving in to sleep in Ben's car at five, holding Ben in my arms and listening to him talk about his fears for the future.

I wanted to say I would buy him the future, that I had enough money to fix it all, but tonight wasn't the right time for it.

My cell began to ring just after seven. Connor. With Ten a short time after. Then Stan, who left a garbled message I didn't understand about dogs with teeth. I called Connor back, and they knew. Everyone knew about the fire from the news.

"Where are you?"

"At the shelter."

"Are you okay? They said you tackled a man with a gun."

"I'm okay."

"And that Ben has been shot?"

"A flesh wound."

I didn't want to talk. I was exhausted and I needed sleep. Ben needed sleep and medical attention. The animals needed to be safe, the shelter rebuilt.

Connor cleared his throat. "Coach is making you a healthy scratch for tonight."

I'd known he would say that; I'd been expecting it. God knew what kind of crap performance I'd put in on the ice with all this happening.

"Okay." I wasn't fighting it.

"I want you back, Max," Connor said. He wasn't ordering or cajoling. Simply and plainly, he was stating a fact. "Next game."

The next game after tonight was in another two days. Did I want hockey more than I wanted to be helping Ben? I opened my mouth to explain I was confused, but Ben snatched the phone from my hand.

"Hello, who is this?" Ben asked. Then he nodded and listened to whatever Connor was saying. "Yep, he'll be there." Then he looked at me as he finished the conversation. "I'll make sure he is, because the Railers have a cup to win."

Chapter Fifteen

Ben

The thing about being bossy is that, generally, the bossy comes back to bite you. Which was why I was now seated in a tiny cubicle in the ER at 6 a.m. having my arm sutured. Max had gotten his bossy on and had called a cab, despite the fact we had kennels and a cattery to empty. All the animals at Crossroads had to be moved to other shelters or taken home by staff and volunteers. Some of the older dogs had been kindly fostered by the workers, but the rest were now in transit to other shelters. Something that I should be overseeing since I was the manager. But no. Mr. Hockey Britches got all demanding and pushy like a boyfriend or something. It was kind of nice, but I wasn't telling Max that.

So here I was, not looking at the stitches being put

into my bicep. Better to look at Max sitting in an ugly chair nursing a cup of coffee. Soot-covered, reeking of smoke, and looking haggard well beyond his age, the man was still a beautiful sight. One that I'd nearly lost.

"Is he done yet?" I asked when I felt a small tug.

Max tipped his head to peer around the ER doctor. "Nope." I squeezed my eyes shut.

Max kept talking, "One time I got forty-two stitches on my forehead. Skate blade. Right here." I peeked at him pointing to a scar right by his hairline. "Went back out and played the rest of the game. Best third period I ever had, hits-wise."

"I thought I recognized you," the doctor said. He and Max then fell into hockey talk. I sat there, mind spinning like a top, exhaustion as heavy as an anvil dropping onto me out of nowhere.

The wound was tended, wrapped, and I was still sluggish, mentally unable to connect to anything aside from the fact I'd been shot. Like, yeah, I knew I'd been shot, because it hurt like a white-hot son-of-a-bitch, but there had been the fire and the police and the organizing of the moving of dogs and cats and... and ...

"Ben?" I looked up from my shaking, bloody hands to see Max leaving his seat, his face a mask of concern. "Do I need to call the doctor back in?"

"No, I just..." I swiped at my wet cheeks with my right hand, just now aware of the tears. "He wanted to kill me. I mean…what did I ever do to that man aside from loving his brother? Dear God."

"I got you."

And he did. He gathered me in his arms and held me as I coughed and cried and tried to make sense of such a vicious hate crime. Rolf had held a gun on his son. His *son!* He'd set fire to my shelter, threatened to kill us all, and for what? A small chunk of property? Sure, that land had some value, but not as much as he thought, I was sure of that. I mean, what the ever-loving hell? Was it hate or greed that had spurred the man to such violence?

"I got you," Max whispered over and over, his big hand moving in soothing circles on my back. "I'll never leave you again."

I buried my face in his neck and clung to him until I couldn't cry any more. I was so shaky and rattled I didn't even feel ashamed about crying. Then Max went into this whole bodyguard-mode thing, talking to the ER doctor for me, promising to stop to pick up the prescription for antibiotics and pain killers, whispering to me where I had to sign to be released, then walking by my side to a waiting cab. My Jeep was still at the shelter. DK had been picked up by his mother and would probably never be allowed to visit me again. And Rolf was in the county lock-up, awaiting bail and assuredly talking to some smarmy lawyer to hasten his release.

The ride home was a hazy blur in the back of a

cab. Max went into Mike's Drugstore to pick up my prescriptions, Max paid the driver, Max steered my frantic aunts into the kitchen then came back and helped me up the stairs, Bucky at our heels, thrilled to be out of his crate.

"I'm kind of into this whole Whitney Houston and Kevin Costner thing we have going on," I teased as he eased me out of my bloody shirt, the wound starting to throb in time with my heart.

"I hope you can sing better than you can dance. Lie down and sleep. I'm going to catch your aunts up, put the dog out, then crash right beside you."

"Okay." There was no energy to say more than that. He pressed a kiss to my cheek, then pulled down the covers on my bed. My man waited by the bed, watching, until I was under the sheets and as comfortable as I could be considering I'd been shot.

"Ben, I'll be right here. You'll be safe. Sleep." He ran his fingers along my jaw. Bucky licked my face. Max turned off the light and pulled the drapes shut. I vaguely heard him calling to the dog. That was all I remembered.

I think Max woke me up to swallow some pills. Then there was heat on both sides of me: man on the left and dog on the right. Nothing wiggled in after that. When I woke up, I was facing my dog. Bucky's tail thumped on the covers as soon as my eyes opened. That made me smile. How could it not?

"Hey, Winter Soldier." I reached out to pet him,

and grimaced. Ouch. Man, flesh wounds hurt big time. Bucky leaped down from the bed and ran in circles while barking, then jumped back up while I was slowly working on sitting up. I heard someone heavy coming up the stairs. Max flew into the room like Satan was nipping at his heels, beautiful eyes wide.

"Why is he barking?" Max asked. Bucky yipped a greeting to my lover, then flopped down next to me.

"He's happy I woke up, I guess."

Max's entire body exhaled in relief. "Scared me. I thought... Well, I thought something had happened or someone—" He shook that off. "Not important. You look better."

"Yeah, I feel better, I guess." I glanced at the clock beside the bed. It was five after five. No wonder I felt rested.

"You want something to eat?"

"In a bit. Now I want a shower and a toothbrush." I pushed to my feet, and Max was right there. "I'm good. Really. It's just a flesh wound," I said in my best Monty Python manner.

He wrapped me in a hug that I stayed in for a long, long time. Bucky snuffled at our legs, doing his best to wiggle in between us.

"Silly pooch." Max smiled, reaching down to scratch Bucky behind an ear. "Go shower. Dinner's covered. We'll eat and then we'll talk."

"I love you." I just wanted to say it because it

needed to be said. Often. Every day. Hell, every hour if possible.

"I love you too." He kissed my brow, then padded off, Bucky opting to stay with me as I showered and pulled on some clean briefs, shorts, and a soft tank top. Lowering and raising my arm hurt. I was not action hero material, I guessed.

When I stepped into my tiny kitchen, a big man was putting plates on the table. Just two plates, but, my gosh, there had to be twenty casserole dishes scattered over the counters. I threw Max a befuddled look. He shrugged.

"The Rose of Beulah congregation has been busy."

"Well, I guess so," I murmured as I studied the pans of lasagna, chicken casserole, tuna casserole, red beans and rice, and macaroni and cheese. Pies and cakes were stacked up by the coffee pot which, praise be to Jesus, was full of fresh coffee.

Max carried a tuna casserole to the table, filled our coffee mugs, and sat down across from me. Bucky slid under the table in case a crumb might roll to the floor.

"Where are the old gals?" I asked after a few mouthfuls.

"Home. I asked them to give us some time to get back on our feet. They said something about planning a bake sale for the shelter."

"That's nice. We're going to need all the money

we can get to fix that fire damage. My insurance is… What? You look funny. Did something happen?"

"Nothing bad. The insurance inspector will be out tomorrow."

Relief swept over me. "Then what? Is it DK?"

"Nope, he's fine. He called from his mom's house and is going to live with her until he goes to college up in Williamsport in the fall. He'll be by to visit, though. I think maybe his mom is a bit worried."

"Can't say as I blame her. I didn't keep him safe at all." My food suddenly tasted off. I shoved the plate to the side. "I didn't keep anyone safe. My animals, my nephew, the shelter Liam and I loved, you."

"Hey, listen, you don't get to carry that guilt burden, you hear me?" He reached over the casserole dish to grab my hand. I glanced from my food to him. He was so stern-looking, but in his gaze there was pain. "If anyone is responsible for what happened, it's me. I should have paid for better security. I should have made sure the gate was locked when we kissed our way through it. Totally on me, not you. You're a victim."

"Paid for *better* security?" Bucky whined under the table, and I placed my dinner on the floor for him, my sight locked on Max. "What do you mean?"

He looked down at his plate. "Oh, well. Yeah. I sort of might have been the mysterious benefactor." When he looked back up all the fire had left his eyes.

Now he just looked sheepish. It was an appealing look on such a gruff hockey player.

I gave him a wobbly smile and threaded my fingers through his. Bucky was loudly snarfing up my dinner, and a warm wind slipped through the screen on the back door.

"I do not think I could love you more than I do right now." His gaze met mine, and there was too much emotion snapping and arcing between us to even begin to put into words. "Let's go back to bed. I need you to love me. Gently wipe the mess outside away for a little while."

"I can do gentle loving."

That was no lie. The man did gentle loving *so* damn well. He eased me into bed, slid me out of my clothes with infinite care of my bandaged bicep, and kissed me all over. Soft little kisses, ticklish and light, to my chest and hips, the soles of my feet and the hollow of my neck. I was languid and loose, whispering soft nothings as he licked at my cock, sucking me deep into his mouth, his fingers traveling up and down my inner thighs. When I reached for him, he softly brushed my hands away.

"This is all for you," he said, his love enveloping us, blocking out the hate that had swept into our lives, as my orgasm slowly built.

When I was on that cusp, he took me in hand, stroking me as he lapped up and down. My eyes closed, fingers digging into the sheets. He sucked skillfully on the head, working the length with a gentle fisting motion.

"Ah, mercy," I gasped as the tremors rolled on and on. Max slithered up over me—as well as a man his size can slither—and kissed a tender path along my jaw to my lips. I pulled his head down, sealing his lips to mine, and worked myself around until we were lying on our sides, gazes touching, Max's thick cock in my hand. "Your turn."

"This was supposed to be just for you," he said, his voice raspy with passion.

"We share everything from now on," I replied, easing my wounded arm up under the pillow as I stroked him base to head. "Orgasms and nosy aunts."

He chuckled, golden eyes glowing. "I'm all up for the orgasms, but the nosy aunts?"

"You get one hundred percent of Ben Worthington and his messed-up life now. That's part of the being in love stuff."

His big body quivered. "I like the sound of that. Even the nosy aunts and the worried dog at the door."

Bucky whined piteously in the hallway, his snuffles at the bottom of the bedroom door making us both laugh.

"You okay with the head stuff?" he asked. I rubbed my palm over the top of his prick. "Yeah, not that head. The head I generally *don't* think with as much as I should."

"I'm coming to terms with it. I hate fearing it, but other than that, I'm good with everything you bring into my life."

No truer words had ever fallen out of my mouth.

THIS GAME, Max sat out. He wasn't happy with that, but given the harrowing situation we'd just gone through, it made sense. Despite how he said he was fine—and me too for that matter—he had to be dealing with some heavy issues. Lord knows I was. Every loud noise made me jump. Someone had dropped a trash can lid at the shelter, and I had nearly dropped to the floor with my hands over my head. Not my proudest moment, but the report of that gunshot would probably haunt me—and Max and DK—for months.

Since I was so edgy, Max hauled me into the press box after getting some clearance from the team. The press box is a special area of the arena set up for the media to report on the game. There's plenty of food for the sportscasters and guests. Tiers of what looked like shelves serving as desks looked down on the ice far below. Laptops and sports journalists filled the seats behind the desks.

Max was in a dark blue suit. I had pulled on a baggy green sweater over a tank top, and a pair of comfortable black jeans. Once we left the arena, I could peel the sweater off.

I'd hoped to be able to just blend into the wood-work, but the press gathered around Max and me, asking far too many questions about the Rolf incident for my liking.

"We're not allowed to talk about it yet," Max said, brushing past the reporters while nudging me along to our seats. A young man, maybe twenty, with thick waves of brown hair, greeted us with a warm smile and a handshake.

"Dad said you'd be in the press box tonight," the handsome kid said as he shook my hand then Max's.

"Dad?" Max asked as he continued holding the young man's hand.

"Oh, sorry. Yeah, I'm Ryker Madsen."

"Well, no shit. Coach talks about you all the time. Says you got great hockey skills."

Looking at Ryker closely, I could see some of Jared Madsen in the young man.

Ryker blushed a bit. "Yeah, he brags a little. I'm okay. Nothing like Ten."

"Few are," Max stated, and no one thought to argue. "This is my boyfriend, Ben."

"Pleasure," I said as Ryker and I shook.

We took our seats and watched the teams warming up on the ice. Poor Max. You could see it was killing him to be up here. I felt a thousand shades of guilty for mucking up yet another thing for him. All this crazy stuff with Rolf was my fault. And he'd just been—

"Hey, no going there," Max whispered beside my ear. "So, Ryker, how goes college life?"

The lanky kid shrugged a shoulder. "Meh. It was okay. I'm transferring to a new campus in Minnesota for next year. My old school wasn't as inclusive as I'd like. The team and campus at Owatonna U. is top-notch for hockey and for the open-minded dean. They've got special dorms for LGBT students, and the team is led by a coach who is adamant about inclusivity."

"Minnesota is hockey heaven. You'll play some great teams," Max said, and the talk went into collegiate hockey.

Ryker went off to grab us some food and drinks and returned with enough grub to feed a hockey team. Jared's son handed off some, then dove into a massive platter of cold cuts, buns, and salads.

"Growing boy," Max whispered to the side.

I nodded in silence. I recalled just how much DK had put away when he'd been with me. I missed him. Damn Rolf to hell for all the chaos and hurt he'd inflicted on so many. I glanced at Max, found him looking at me with concern, and shoved Rolf and his asshattery to a far corner of my mind. I refused to let him ruin another moment of my life.

Talk flowed freely with Ryker. He was an affable young man—clever, funny, and quite charming.

The game looked different from up here, the players smaller and harder to distinguish. Thankfully, the Jumbotron was right there, and so I got to watch the huge face of a famous singer belt out the national anthem as I nibbled on some wheat crackers and strong cheese.

The arena was alive with excitement. All the fans were loud and cheering until the Raptors scored quickly in the first two minutes of the game. Things grew quiet, a bit, but the chants of "Let's go Railers" rolled steadily around the packed rink. Then the team from Arizona put on their nasty faces and went after Tennant Rowe like hyenas after a wounded gazelle. I'd seen this happen to our star player in Washington, as well as on the Pittsburgh team. Any highly skilled forward was targeted. Take the goal-scorers out and you stand a better chance of winning the game. Makes total sense, even if it is barbaric.

Ten couldn't catch a pass or set one up without a defender on him, mauling him, shoving and battering him. No matter how many penalties for hooking, holding, or high-sticking the refs called, the Raptors, particularly a huge Finn, Aarni Lankinen, continued to abuse Rowe. Which infuriated everyone on the ice and the man seated on my left.

"Those fuckers," Max snarled when we were deep into the third period, down 3–0, and Tennant had just had his nose bloodied by yet another high stick. "I was supposed to be down there protecting Ten. Coach asked me to keep him safe."

Yet another miserable thing I was going to heap

onto the refuse pile Rolf had created. The game ended with an empty-net goal by the Raptors, a shut-out for the Arizona goalie, and probably several stitches in the bridge of Tennant Rowe's nose. There was no consoling Max.

"I'm going to grind those pretty boys into mother-fucking paste next game," he snarled as we sat in an empty press box, staring at the Zamboni grooming the ice.

"Pound them good," Ryker mumbled in agreement.

Chapter Sixteen

Max

Payback started as soon as I hit the ice in warmups before the next game. I'd already given notice in my off-day interview with the press that I was there to protect Ten and there was no chance of our opponents treating him as they had in the last game. Every team took their chances this late in the Cup, but if this was going to be bloody, then it would be me calling the shots.

"Do you have a message for them?" one of the press interviewers asked. I don't know who it was, but I was ready for the question.

I faced the camera. I knew what the press wanted, what the team needed, and I was ready to give it to them.

"I'm coming for you."

And now, skating in lazy figure eights on the ice, stick handling a puck as the arena shook to the bass of Shakira, I was getting very close to the center line, catching opponents' eyes, letting them know I was watching them. Whether this psychology worked or not, I didn't care—they were on a warning. I flicked the puck onto my stick and bounced it there, standing right at center and staring at the Raptors. A couple of their D-Men skated close and tried to front, but let's face it, I was the one with something to prove, and I wasn't letting any kind of intimidation push me off-track.

Coach was way more animated tonight; he was either pissed at our loss in the last game or someone had slipped him a drink. He called out the starting lineup. I was up first in defense, and Ten was there on the first line. I knew my job.

I lasted three seconds. We lost the first faceoff, but that didn't matter. I shoved my way into Aarni Lanki-nen's face and dropped gloves, and that was it; with the roar of the crowd in my ears, I wanted retribution and to teach Lankinen a lesson.

He knew it was coming, his stick on the floor, his gloves off, and he was a big guy. Maybe an inch shorter than me, he was solid with muscle and fast on his skates. And there was the light of anticipation in his eyes. He wanted this as much as I did. A win for him would be the period to the shit he'd dealt out to Ten. A win for me was justice.

We didn't dance. I was in there, a solid one-two to his cheekbone, and he countered with his own throw which caught my chin and sent my head back sharply. A lesser man would have given up, maybe dragged Lankinen to the ice and sat on him, but I was angry.

Desperate because they'd targeted Ten, guilty I hadn't been there to stop it, furious at Rolf and what he'd done to the shelter and more importantly to Ben, it all boiled up inside me, a rush of anger and pain and lethal accuracy. One punch, just in the right spot, and Lankinen was on the ground, gripping my shirt and taking me with him. Sprawled like that, I had the scarlet of anger still bright in me, and I tried for more punches, only stopping after two officials and my own team pulled me off. There was blood on my hands, blood on his face, and that was me done.

Message sent.

I skated away from Lankinen spread-eagled on the ice, and as I skated to the box for the inevitable penalty, I passed Ten and fist bumped him. The kid had the widest grin but was clearly trying to hide it. Jared said nothing to me—he didn't even look my way —but he tapped my shoulder when I was out of the penalty box, and that was enough.

The game was ours from that moment, and we played with fire. Ben wasn't there tonight—there was too much to do at the center, and I'd encouraged him to stay away. I wasn't sure I wanted him to watch my blood lust.

We won by three goals, two of those from a still-grinning Tennant Rowe.

We were tied in the Stanley Cup final—the goddamn Railers were tied. Three games left, and if we could win two of them we could be the fucking champions.

Two more wins was all we needed.

The next game was back in Arizona, and that was the only bastard thing about this final match-up; away games meant a long-ass flight.

But you know what? Ben stayed up for that game and watched us win by a slim margin in our opposing team's barn. We were flying.

We could win this Cup at home. All we needed was one more game.

WALKING into the shelter was like coming home. I had the code for the gate memorized, and didn't need to buzz for entry, and no one blinked at me standing inside the entrance staring at what was left of the office building.

Ben stalked over to me from the kennel area, paperwork under his arm and his expression unreadable.

"Was this you?" he thumbed over his shoulder at the men huddled in a group talking and pointing at the offices. They all wore hard hats, and there was a *lot* of pointing. Of course it was me. The day after the fire, I'd asked my agent to source the best builder, the best architect, and I wanted it done now. I'd never asked for anything like that before, never used my money to grease the wheels of city hall, but who could have known the head of the agriculture department was a hockey fan? Spaces in a box for him and his hockey-loving daughter, and he hurried through whatever needed to be done.

But I couldn't read Ben's expression, and I wondered if maybe this thing I'd done was so completely wrong it would never be right. I wasn't entirely sure how to answer the question, and he was up in my face before I thought of the right words.

"What do you mean?" I stood my ground.

"They want to start clearance today. Three weeks and they think the center will be back again." He didn't sound excited, or angry; I think if I was going to sum it up, it would be that he was blindsided.

I couldn't hold it in. He could be pissed if he wanted to, but I was proud of what I'd done for him, and I was proud of the Railers fans who had donated at the game last night and raised over thirty thousand dollars for the shelter. He couldn't know that yet—I had the final tally in my pocket, along with personal checks from half the team. It was easy enough to get the shelter rebuilt and enhanced. Maybe even hire some more staff at this location and possibly open a second location, one where I could work alongside him after hockey.

The team all knew Ben and loved what he did. What was there not to love?

He cradled my face, and then he smiled, just a little smile, and understanding filled his eyes.

"Thank you," he said.

We kissed, and then hugged, and I knew I'd done the right thing. Now if only I could think more about my life post hockey, a life with Ben, then maybe I'd begin to focus on the percentage that was positive, on the fact Doctor Warner kept telling me the bleed was unlikely to happen again.

After all, who knew how long a man's life would be? It was what you did with that life that mattered.

TENSION WAS high in the room. Coach had morphed back into Quiet Guy, but he was focused and determined, and he took a stance in the locker room that was implacable.

"They'll be gunning for Ten. They're a team as desperate as us." He didn't need to say that, we all knew it as a fact, but to hear the words made everything so damn real.

Right here, in front of seventeen thousand Railers fans who'd stuck with this expansion team, we could take home hockey's biggest prize.

The game started slow. I want to say it was cautious, with us not wanting to make stupid mistakes and them holding back to avoid penalties, but it was more like we were sizing each other up. I'd already gone face to face with Lankinen. We'd exchanged chirps, got up in each other's spaces, but tonight wasn't about fighting.

Tonight, Coach needed me to skate the hell out of this and generate chances for our forwards. We had to play *right*.

The first period was scoreless, and the second had only two minutes left on the clock when the Raptors found a way past Stan. I wasn't on the ice, part of the next D-pair going over the boards, but even if I had been I wouldn't have been able to stop the lucky bounce that clipped Adler and went in off Stan's knee.

Stan turned to his pipes, didn't react to the goal, but I could imagine what he was doing. Asking for their help, apologizing—who knew exactly.

"It's okay, boys," Coach said in the locker room. "It's one goal."

One goal was one too many, and we all knew it. Twenty minutes stood between us and winning the cup. We lost this game and we'd have to go back to Arizona.

"Arizona is too hot," I said in a lull in the conversation. "I'm not going back there."

Silence, and then one by one the guys agreed.

The last period of twenty started well enough, Ten was all over the fucking ice, and the resulting goal from his fast skates and even quicker hands was beautiful.

Tied. With ten minutes left.

Still tied with three minutes to go.

The Raptors had used their timeout, we still had ours, and Coach called it. I knew why; it wasn't to discuss strategy, but to give Ten's line a breather. The kid was on fire. He leaned over to us, huddled around him, and he said one thing he knew would give us the last push.

"Finish this already."

The clock counted down, and we were so evenly matched that there were limited chances. The Raptors had three shots on goal in one minute, and a rebound, all dealt with by a deadly efficient Stan. We matched them at their end.

One minute. Still tied. Sixty seconds on this game, and there was no way through.

Their star forward was heading for our goal. I was there, skating backward, blocking him, the puck leaving his stick and hitting my thigh as I leaned to block it.

Adler collected the fallen puck on his stick, and sharply passed it to Ten, who crossed it to Larson, and then everything seemed to slow. I could read the play; it was something I'd seen Ten and Addison do before, cycling the puck between them as the seconds counted down.

The first shot was blocked by their goalie, but he

couldn't collect it and instead it was right on Ten's stick, and the kid went down on one knee, slapping the puck so fast no one had a chance of stopping it.

The lamp lit, the home crowd was on their feet, and we gripped Ten hard.

We were a goal up with twenty-three seconds on the clock.

Now it was our job to keep them shut out to every goal possibility for every heartbeat of those seconds.

When the klaxon sounded to signal the end of the game, we'd won.

The game.

The series.

The goddamn Stanley Cup.

I was a Stanley Cup Champion, and it was everything I'd ever wanted.

But. Up there, with the families, Ben was watching this, and I realized I actually had him as well. Winning the Cup had been the only goal in my life, but now it was Ben who was my everything.

This was my last ever professional hockey game, and what a way to go.

The chaos was loud and manic, and the pile we made with Stan at the bottom was full of laughter and shouts, and then we moved back in a huddle, Stan lifting Ten up and swinging him around. We shook hands with the opposition, who looked exhausted but took the time to congratulate us. That was the thing about hockey. Under it all, most teams respected each other.

Except for Lankinen who cursed at me under his breath and called me names I chose to ignore. Fucker.

We hugged and whooped and only stopped when they rolled out the red carpets for the Cup. Then it all became so serious.

We grouped around Connor, and then he skated over after the announcement of the win. He took the Cup, and the look on his face was priceless. They'd said it couldn't be done, that this expansion team was made up of cast-offs but they'd been wrong. So wrong.

Connor passed it to Ten. We knew he would—the kid was a star, the shining light of the Railers, and a future Hall-of-Famer for sure. I watched my team skate with the Cup individually, and then it was my turn. I took it from Adler, who was grinning manically.

"There you go, old man!" he shouted in my ear.

I took the weight of the Cup; it was heavy, but God, skating my lap of the rink with it, it began to feel as light as a feather. I stopped briefly where I knew Ben was, and gestured with the Cup, hoping he'd see what I did. Then I saw him, right by the ice, and he was grinning and clapping, and there it was.

The Stanley Cup in my hands, the man I loved right there where I could see him, and the arena ringing with cheers.

Life couldn't get any better.

THEY LET family onto the ice, and that included Ben, and I hugged him, refused to let him go, posing for pictures with the team, then acting up for the cameras recording all this. Adler had started some kind of weird shimmy dance, and I was so up for that, joining him and Ten in a weird dance-off even as Connor joined us and pulled me aside. He'd done the same for everyone, and it was my turn.

"Hell of a game," he shouted over the cacophony of noises around us.

"Hell of a series, Cap," I shouted back.

He clapped me on the back. This was my last game, my last time on the ice like this. The excitement was intense and Ben was right there. I skated toward him, held out a hand, wanting to touch him.

And then everything went black.

Chapter Seventeen

Max

The voice was soft but insistent, calling my name, the light so bright I shoved it away. At least, I thought I did, but I couldn't feel my hand connecting with anything, and I hurt. Everywhere.

"He's waking up," that voice said, and there was relief in the tone. There was nothing but quiet. What had happened to the roar of the crowd, the shouting, the celebration? Where had it gone?

"Hey, Max?"

That was Ben's voice, and I wanted to say something. *What happened? Why am I warm? My head hurts.*

None of it happened, and I was tired. I closed my eyes again. A nap would help.

. . .

THE NAP LEFT me feeling sick. At least I thought it was the nap. Someone held my head when I was sick. I heard Ben's voice, and I focused on him completely.

Ben? I asked, but the words weren't coming. *Ben, I love you. What happened?*

THE LIGHT LESSENED, the pain in my head with it, and I wasn't feeling sick. That was the appraisal of my situation when I next opened my eyes.

"Hey," Ben said to me immediately.

"Wh'appen?" I managed, and this time the words worked.

"You had a bleed," Ben said, softly and without explanation.

Shit. I couldn't have. I'd believed in the positives. Why had it gone wrong?

"It wasn't a major bleed, but Doc Warner was here, and he… It's too complicated, but you're okay. You're *going* to be okay. The fire, the stress, the game, the hit you got from that D-man, the pressure of the final, the win…the Doctor thinks it was enough to bring this on. It wasn't a stroke, just a small bleed. You made the papers—collapsing at the final was kinda dramatic."

I wanted him to stop talking, I could hear the fear in his voice, and I wanted to address that.

"I love you," I managed to say, my tongue thick, my words a little slurred. He gripped my hand, then he kissed me. I felt his touch, I responded, and I felt his kiss.

I wasn't broken. I could get back from this.

I WAS in the hospital for three days, mostly under observation, and after day one I was feeling good enough to get out of there. By day two, I was irritable. Ben gave me news about the shelter, showed me pictures, told me about donations and the puppies moving back and how Stan and Erik had taken two of the labs and a crossbreed no one could tell what it was at all. Apparently, it was so tiny it could sit in Stan's hand, and had made friends with his cat.

"So much for Stan wanting a guard dog," Ben finished.

"I want to go home," I announced, as if I hadn't been listening to what he said at all.

"Westy said he's checked in on your apartment—"

"No," I interrupted, "your place, our home."

I thought he might cry then, and I squeezed his hand. "I love you."

He kissed my forehead gently. "And I love you."

THE DOCTOR WAS blunt and to the point. I'd experienced a small bleed, nothing too dramatic, and he'd shut it down, and that was probably the last of it now. The weakness he'd never been able to pinpoint had exposed itself horribly, and that was the end of things. The positive percentage I had to cling on was higher, apparently. Ben seemed relieved, but at no point in the explanation did he let go of my hand, not once.

I had my moment in the spotlight. Ben kept the paper—Stanley Cup Champion Collapses on Ice at Final—and had links to YouTube videos of the moment I'd collapsed. All I could think was I'd gone to the ice as gracelessly as if I'd been punched out. It was embarrassing.

The third day was going home day, Ben's aunts fussing, most of the team waiting at the small house.

Right in the middle of the tiny front room sat the thing I'd been fighting for. The Cup.

We took photos, alone, with the team, but the best bit was when they went and I was left with Ben.

Just as it should be.

Epilogue

Ben

I was beginning to think I could relate to all those new parents, the ones who say they wake up and listen to the baby monitor to make sure Junior is breathing. Three weeks after Max collapsed on the ice, I was still doing that. Jolting awake in the middle of the night, heart pounding in my ribcage while some foggy nightmare of me burying Max next to Liam faded away. I'd reach over and lay a hand on his chest or hold my ragged breath until I could hear him breathing. I wasn't sure if I'd ever get over it. Guess the fear of loss was embedded too deep, like a splinter in my soul that could never be extracted.

Fear and love kept me tight to his side, or as tight as I could be and not be hanging off his back like a monkey. Every time he went off somewhere to do something, I worried until he came back. Thank God, he had the sense not to drive. I was happy to be his taxi. Sometimes I'd tease him about him being Miss Daisy just to get his back up, but I was happy to take him where he needed to be. Which, now that he'd retired, was not much of anywhere in particular.

"Earth to Ben," Max said, pulling me from myself. I glanced to the right. He was riding with his window down, looking a great deal like Bucky in the back, clean country air blowing in his joyful face as we rode out to see yet another possible new home.

"Lost in the stuff," I said, and reached for the stereo to turn up Earth, Wind & Fire.

"Bad things stay in the past, remember?"

"Yep."

That was easier said than done, since we still had to deal with Rolf and all that legality. His trial was several months off, and he was out on bail. There was a restraining order in place to keep me, his family, my aunts, and the shelter safe, but still…

"Okay, so you're not thinking about dickhead."

"I am not thinking about dickhead." I chuckled. "Get back on that app and make sure the realtor sent us the right directions."

I'd never been this far into Lancaster County. I'd only come out here a couple of times with my aunts to do touristy things like shop and try to catch a peek at the Amish, who have a vibrant community in this county. We'd rolled into some beautiful farmland, and had passed a horse and buggy, which Max had been thrilled to see.

"On it," my boyfriend said, flipping around on his cell phone as we cruised past green pastures dotted with sheep or dairy cattle.

This was where Max wanted to live. Away from the city. Breathing fresh air and opening a second no-kill shelter. One that we would run together. Every time I thought about our new life out in the farmland, together, I felt sick with nerves and giddy with love.

"Another couple miles on 340 until we come into Intercourse."

He snickered at the town name, just as he did every time he read it. I loved hearing him laugh, even if it was kind of childish.

"And once we've passed Intercourse?"

"We have a cigarette." He roared at that one. I shook my head and tried to hide my chuckle. "Oh, I amuse myself. Okay, all kidding aside, we jump onto 772. Maybe we'll get to see a covered bridge out here. They're all over the place."

"Maybe." I followed his directions, my inner-city boy starting to feel a little antsy out among all this farmland and roads with no street signs. "Are you sure you want to be so far out here? There's nothing but cows and corn."

"Yeah, it's perfect, isn't it? No neighbors, no zoning boards, no traffic or drugs or crime."

"That's true." I also suspected he was trying to get

me as far from Rolf's line of sight as he possibly could. "I guess having a shelter out here would be good."

"Yep. We can maybe even take in farm animals out here. Goats are cool. Let's take in some needy goats."

I pulled up to a stop sign that linked four dirt roads and gave him a look. "Goats. And what do we know about goats?"

"We'll learn all we need to know on the internet." He leaned in to kiss me. Bucky wiggled up to slather both of our faces. "See, even Bucky thinks we should do goats. Or a cow. I could milk a cow."

"I could see you skipping to a barn with your milk pail every morning."

It was said kiddingly, but I really *could* see him doing that. I could envision us making this new shelter into something bigger and better. A place for farm animals in need as well as small pets.

"I think we need a big cock, too," I said, and waited for a wise-ass comment. It never came because Max was reading something on his phone.

"Huh," was all he said. "The Railers picked up a new backup goalie. Some kid from the Raptors, backed up their starter. Bryan Delaney is his name. Shit, he's just a sucking pup. We'll have all kinds of fun with him and that sweet little baby face when he walks into the dressing room for the— Well, shit."

He lowered his cell and gave me the saddest damn

look. I reached for his hand and gave the big mitt a hard squeeze.

"I'm going to miss hockey," he confessed.

"I know. But, you'll be so busy milking cows and playing with goats and loving me that you won't have time to miss it much."

"Yeah, that's right. We're starting over, both of us. Maybe we can name the farm-slash-shelter New Beginnings."

I nodded. "That's a fine name."

Max smiled proudly. "Just imagine the shots for the calendar we can get on a farm."

"You're going to be on the cover with me, right?"

"On the cover? Oh yeah, I'd like that. Sure. You, me, Bucky, and the new goat."

That sounded just about perfect. Even the goat part.

THE END

Next for the Railers

Goal Line (Harrisburg Railers Hockey #6)

Fear and sadness mark Bryan's life, can Gatlin show him that you have to trust before you can love?

Gatlin Pearce is creeping up on thirty-eight and is still single. It's not that he wants to be alone, it's just that he's too damn old to be in clubs filled with glittery gay boys who can't even tell him who the Rolling Stones are. Better to just spend his evenings at Hard Score Ink - his tattoo and artwork shop - creating masterpieces on human flesh, listening to the Railers games, and nursing a cold beer.

His solitary life is about to end when Bryan Delaney, the new Railers backup goalie, shows up at his shop looking for new artwork for his helmet. There's some sort of sad story in those beautiful eyes of Bryan's, and Gatlin finds himself more than a little infatuated with the tender new goalie.

Bryan Delaney leaves home at fifteen to live with a billet family. He just wishes that he could have escaped his alcoholic father and strictly devout mother earlier. Drafted to the Arizona Raptors he finds a new family, and his first love affair, even if that relationship is marked with violence.

Being traded to the Railers is a shock to the system but the team isn't like any other he's ever played on and they truly seem to care about him. It's only when he meets artist Gatlin, with their shared love of music and hockey, that he realizes how much help he needs to escape the past.

Harrisburg Railers

Owatonna U Hockey

Arizona Raptors

Boston Rebels

LA Storm

Chesterford Coyotes - Young Adult

Free Reads

Please note - in all of these free stories, there will be some spoilers for the main series books.

Railers Short Stories

Volume 1 | Volume 2

LA Storm

Sparkle

The Colts - AHL Short Stories

Pucks & Percentages

Breakaway

Making the Save

Standalone

Waiting for Christmas

Harrisburg Railers

When hockey wunderkind Tennant Rowe meets his new coach, he knows he's in trouble. Jared Madsen is nine years older than Tennant, impossibly attractive, and — worst of all — his brother's off-limits best friend. Is their chemistry worth the risk?

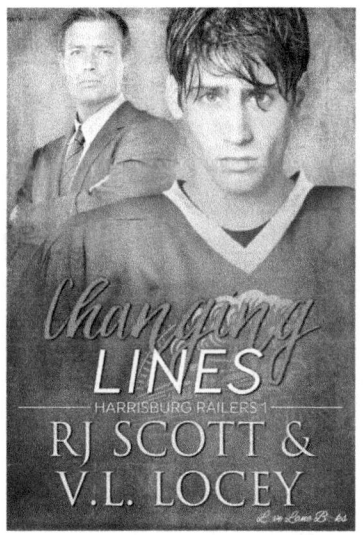

Changing Lines (Railers 1)

Can Tennant show Jared that age is just a number, and that love is all that matters?

The Rowe Brothers are famous hockey hotshots, but as the youngest of the trio, Tennant has always had to play against his brothers' reputations. To get out of their shadows, and against their advice, he accepts a trade to the Harrisburg Railers, where he runs into Jared Madsen. Mads is an old family friend and his brother's one-time teammate. Mads is Tennant's new coach. And Mads is the sexiest thing he's ever laid eyes on.

Jared Madsen's hockey career was cut short by a fault in his heart, but coaching keeps him close to the game. When Ten is traded to the team, his carefully organized world is thrown into chaos. Nine years his junior and his best friend's brother, he knows Ten is strictly off-limits, but as soon as he sees Ten's moves, on and off the ice, he knows that his heart could get him into trouble again.

Changing Lines

Harrisburg Railers (Hockey Romance)

1. Changing Lines
2. First Season
3. Deep Edge
4. Poke Check
5. Last Defense
6. Goal Line
7. Neutral Zone
8. Hat Trick
9. Save The Date
10. Baby Makes Three

Railers Volume 1 | Railers Volume 2 | Railers Volume 3 | Railers Volume 4

Meet the men of Owatonna University's hockey team

Ryker (Owatonna U, 1)

Ryker

Ryker is hockey royalty, Jacob is a poor country boy. Can two vastly different people find common ground and become the men they want to be?

Ryker comes from a long line of championship-winning hockey players. Playing college hockey to develop his game is his only focus, and nothing will stand in the way of him working to become the best player. He has no room for relationships, people who point out his flaws, or anyone who calls him on his dreams. He certainly has no place for love, and meeting Jacob is nothing but a useful distraction on the side. After all trying to get his Owatonna Eagles teammate into bed is less work and more play. When tragedy rocks his family, his charmed life crumbles, and the only person he can turn to is the same one who claims to hate him.

Jacob Benson has only known hard work and stifling conservative values his whole life. Born and raised in the small rural community of Eden Crossing, Minnesota, he's the only son of a hard-working but struggling dairy farming family. Jacob is using his skills in hockey to finance his way to an agricultural science degree. These four years at Owatonna U. will probably be the only time he has to enjoy life, gain acceptance about his sexuality, and live openly before his inevitable return to the farm. Running into a pretty rich boy like Ryker Madsen is putting a damper on his enjoyment of life away from home. Ryker's flip, conceited, carefree attitude grates on Jacob's every nerve. So why, if Ryker is everything he dislikes, does he want nothing more than to explore the sinful dreams that his annoying teammate stars in every night?

Ryker

Owatonna U Hockey (Hockey Romance)

1. Ryker

Arizona Raptors

Coast to Coast (Arizona Raptors 1)

Coast To Coast

When opposites attract, this bottom-of-the-league team will never be the same again.

A stipulation in his father's will forces Mark back into the arms of a family that disowned him and leaves him one-third owner of a hockey team facing financial ruin. He doesn't even watch hockey, let alone like it, and wants nothing more than to head back to New York. Then there's the new coach, a stubborn, opinionated, irritating man with superiority issues and questionable music taste. Butting heads with Rowen becomes the new normal, but it comes with passionate debate and an all-consuming lust.

Challenged to rebuild one of the worst teams in the league into a future cup contender, Rowen can't pass up the opportunity. Never in his twenty years of hockey has he ever seen a team managed so badly or coached players overflowing with resentment and bigotry. Yet there's something about this team and this city that compels him to roll up his sleeves and start dismantling. If only Mark, one of three siblings who now own the Raptors, wasn't so damned rock-headed yet so damned appealing his job might be easier. It doesn't look like either is willing to give in, but one night in a dark, desert hotel changes everything.

Coast To Coast

Arizona Raptors (Hockey Romance)

1. Coast To Coast
2. Across the Pond
3. Shadow and Light
4. Sugar and Ice
5. School and Rock

Boston Rebels

Top Shelf (Boston Rebels 1)

Acting on the attraction to his best friend's brother has always been off the table for Xander until a passionate hookup with Mason at a beach resort begins a love affair that burns long after summer ends.

Mason specializes in assisting same-sex couples on their journey to becoming parents and fighting every rule that blocks his way in the stuck-in-the-past agency that hired him. Living in his brother's pool house is rent-free, and every cent he earns he saves for his dream—that one day he'd have his own company helping others. The downside is that he has to see his annoying brother every day, the upside is that his brother's teammates from the Boston Rebels make regular visits. The eye candy that passes Mason's window is almost enough to make him consider dating a hockey player, but not just any player though. Ever since Xander—his brother's childhood friend—came out as gay at a press conference, Mason's puppy love has turned into a burning attraction he can no longer ignore.

Hockey has been one of Xander's main focuses since he was old enough to balance on skates. Well, hockey and Mason Kingsley, but Mason was always unattainable. Now that he's about to see thirty candles on his birthday cake and is no longer hiding the fact he's gay, he's ready to find a soul mate to make his life complete. A summer vacation is just what he needs to have time to think, but when the Boston Rebels arriving in paradise with Mason in tow, thinking is the last thing he needs. One torrid night under a balmy moon and rules about not messing with his best friend's brother vanish on a warm, tropical breeze.

Summer romances don't generally last past Labor Day, but with the new season about to begin Xander and Mason are going to have to face the world and decide if their love is real enough to withstand everything.

Boston Rebels

Lost In Boston (Free Prequel Novella)

1. Top Shelf

2. Back Check
3. Snowed
4. Royal Lines
5. Blade
6. Rental

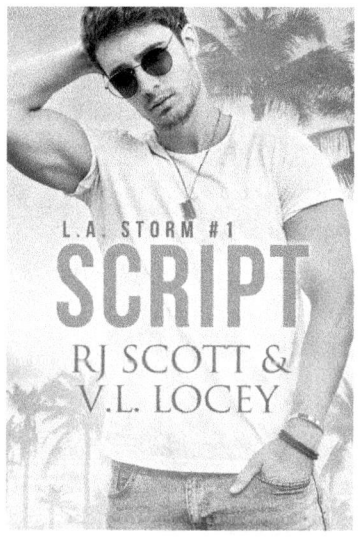

Script (LA Storm, 1)

Script

Hollywood A-lister Finn might be Canadian, but he needs Cameron to show him how to hockey.

Actor Finn Kerrigan is at a crossroads. After growing up a soap star, then starring in a hugely successful trilogy of action movies, he's finally given the chance to read a heartfelt and passionate script that could change his life forever. The role would be enough for people to see him as a serious actor, and maybe even win him an award or two (and no, a golden raspberry award for his action movies doesn't count). Once established as a serious actor he's sure he can come out of the closet and finally live his truth.

When he lies to get the part of a hockey player on a struggling team, he suddenly has nowhere to hide. He might be Canadian, but the last time he skated he was ten, and no, he doesn't have hockey in his blood. With only a month until filming starts, he about to be exposed, but partnered with a player who's supposed to be giving him tips, he doesn't realize how many of his secrets will come to light. Falling in lust, one heated kiss at a time, is inevitable, but giving Cameron up at the end of the shoot could break his heart.

Cameron Chavkin is the face of the LA Storm. And the body, and the hair, and the smile. He's at the prime of his career, men and women want to be with him, and he's skating better than he ever has before. His house sits next to a famous rock star's mansion, his garage is filled with expensive cars, and he's even been asked to mentor a once-famous actor in a new hockey movie. Life is pretty sweet. Until the bad boy of hockey meets Finn, a man on the edge with more secrets than Cameron has endorsements. Knowing better than to get involved, Cameron is swept up despite himself, and when it's time to say goodbye to the Storm's most eligible bachelor is finding it hard to follow the script.

Script

LA Storm

1. Script
2. Second
3. Shield
4. Spiral

Off The Ice (Chesterford Coyotes, 1)

Off The Ice

A coming-of-age love story with high school, hockey rivalry, friendship, family, and coming out.

Soren's life changes in an instant when he and his younger brother are adopted by hockey royalty. Making sense of his new life is hard enough, but when he's enrolled in a private school it means facing a whole new set of problems. Navigating friendship, family, and hockey is one thing, but being attracted to the boy who vexes him is a whole new thing.

Felix has a reputation to protect. He's the kid who seems to have everything but looks can be deceiving. Spinning lies about his perfect life, he's created a fantasy world that even he has started to believe. Only, it's not long before everything crumbles, all of his pretty lies are revealed, and only his closest rival sees through his pain and stands by him.

Fighting is easy, friendship is hard, but love is everything.

Off The Ice

Chesterford Coyotes

1. Off The Ice
2. On Thin Ice
3. *Dance on Ice*

Also By RJ Scott

For a full list of ebooks and links please scan the code above
or visit rjscott.co.uk/rjbooks

Meet RJ Scott

RJ discovered romance in books at a very young age and realized that if there wasn't romance on the page, she could create it in her head. With over one hundred and fifty books published, she is a full time author of gay romance.

She lives and works out of her home in the beautiful English countryside, spends her spare time reading, watching films, and enjoying time with her family.

The last time she had a week's break from writing she didn't like it one little bit and has yet to meet a box of chocolates she couldn't defeat.

www.rjscott.co.uk | rj@rjscott.co.uk

NEWSLETTER - rjscott.co.uk/rjnews

facebook.com/author.rjscott

x.com/Rjscott_author

instagram.com/rjscott_author

amazon.com/author/rj-scott

bookbub.com/authors/rj-scott

goodreads.com/rjscott

pinterest.com/rjscottauthor

Also By VL Locey

For a full list of ebooks and links please scan the code above
or visit vllocey.com/stories-from-vl-locey

Meet V.L. Locey

V.L. Locey loves worn jeans, yoga, belly laughs, walking, reading and writing lusty tales, Greek mythology, the New York Rangers, comic books, and coffee.

(Not necessarily in that order.)

She shares her life with her husband, her daughter, one dog, two cats, a flock of assorted domestic fowl, and two Jersey steers.

When not writing spicy romances, she enjoys spending her day with her menagerie in the rolling hills of Pennsylvania with a cup of fresh java in hand.

vllocey.com
vicki@vllocey.com

Newsletter - vllocey.com/newsletter

facebook.com/V.L.Locey

x.com/vllocey

instagram.com/vl_locey

bookbub.com/authors/v-l-locey

goodreads.com/vllocey

pinterest.com/vllocey

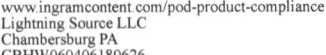